Dead Silence

A Swanson Herbinko Mystery

Paris

Bathsheba Monk

Blue Heron Book Works

Allentown

ISBN: 9968177-2-7
ISBN-13: 978-0-9968177-2-1

Cover Design by Angie Zambrano
Stylist Rose Ellen Moore of RC Moore For the Unique Individual
Cover photo by Paul Heller
Cover model Angela DeAngelo

Blue Heron Book Works, LLC
Allentown, PA 18104

www.blueheronbookworks.com

bathshebamonk.com

To Lizzie and Michel Brown, wherever you are

Table of Contents

Chapter 1

Skinny People Suck

My private investigator, Dick, insists that I meet him at the new vegan restaurant on Beacon Hill, the Holy Bean. And he's late. Unusual for Dick and I wouldn't ordinarily care, except have you ever seen a vegan? They are incredibly skinny. The ten people milling around waiting for the hostess to seat us are skinny. The hostess is skinny. The other waiting patrons are sitting on each other's laps, squeezing two to a chair and laughing about it, while I spread my cushiony bottom on one chair which squeaks discourteously, cross my legs and tug Devil Dog, my dachshund, closer so we take up less space.

The hostess seats everyone else then frowns, sizing me up—correctly—as a meat eater then approaches, her tiny body completely hidden behind a gigantic menu. "Are you alone?"

I know she means am I dining alone, but the fact is, in the cosmic sense of the word, I *am* alone. The love of my life, Hidalgo, was murdered six months ago. My uncles, the only family I have, are attending the Cordon Bleu cooking school in Paris and they are determined to stay there, ignoring my emails and texts begging them to come home, instead telling me to go on Expedia and check out cheap flights across "the pond" as they so anachronistically call the Atlantic Ocean. Even the house I was raised in is gone, seized by eminent domain and knocked over to make way for a super highway into Boston. I start to tear up, because, OMG! I *am* alone! Devil Dog growls at the hostess.

"He can't stay here if he makes noise," the hostess says, lifting up her stick-like arm to capture some stray blond hairs that have escaped her barrette.

"He doesn't make noise," I say. I yank on his chain and he yaps. "And I'm not alone. I'm waiting for a friend." And just when I was pondering whether Dick is technically a friend, an employee or a sub-contractor who works for me when I'm handling a particularly messy divorce, he walks through the door.

"It's about time," I say.

Here's the thing about Dick: he's probably the best private investigator in Massachusetts, he looks like a middle-aged model, one of those steel-haired craggy guys pushing Colloidal Silver in AARP magazine, he keeps his body in shape by running five miles every other day, hitting the gym for weight training on the odd days, yoga like *all* the time, and he keeps his mind in shape by reading "The Tibetan Book of the Dead" and Leo Tolstoy. He knows something about everything, which is a handy trait to have in someone helping you find things out about people, but frankly? All of his perfection makes me feel less perfect myself.

"Swanson!" Dick bends down to pat Devil Dog, who regards Dick's uncharacteristic friendliness with suspicion but still can't resist a head scratch and let's himself be petted.

Traitor.

"How ya doing boy?"

The reason he wouldn't take Howie Carr, the greyhound I rescued from Suffolk Downs last summer, is because Dick is one of the most fastidious persons on the planet. One stray hair on his Armani jacket ruins his day. "I think you got some dog hair on you," I tell Dick.

"Do I?" He stands up, rubs his hands together and smiles dreamily at the hostess, who seems to know him and is smiling back. "Hi, Ginger."

I groan. Of course the hostess in a vegan restaurant would be called Ginger. Or Rosemary. Or Sage.

"Right this way, Dick. I saved you a corner booth," she walks briskly into the dining room carrying the ridiculous over-sized menus, turning to give me an any friend of Dick's is a friend of mine smile with her big horsey teeth. Devil Dog walks haughtily, accepting the coos and greetings of the patrons, who seem to actually love animals, just not on the end of a fork.

I squeeze into the booth, clearly sized for non-carnivores and pick up the menu. A couple rows of tofu and tempeh entrees, lots of beans and bulgur wheat. Twenty flavors of lemonade, sweetened with agave. When the waitress asks what we want to drink, I ask her if I can have strawberry lemonade, "with honey, though, not agave." What the heck is agave? Vegans aren't the only ones with rules about what they won't eat. I won't eat something if I don't know what it is.

The waitress freezes with her pencil over her pad, then looks to Dick for help, but he's staring at the ceiling with an idiotic grin on his face. I glance up to see what he finds so fascinating on the ceiling. Nothing. I snap my fingers in his face.

"This is a *vegan* restaurant," the waitress finally manages.

I nod. "So?"

"Honey is made by *bees*!"

"We're not *eating* the bees, are we? I mean, you don't grind up the bees and stick them in the honey, do you?"

"That's not the *point*," she says, clearly flustered at having a non-believer in the restaurant.

"It's just a plant, Swanson," Dick says. "From Mexico."

Definitely the wrong thing to say. Hidalgo was from Mexico, too. I close my eyes so I don't start to cry. Jeez, when will I ever get over this?

"We don't want to use any products that have used animals as our slaves to produce them," the waitress finally remembers her training.

Her eyes redden at the thought of it. She sticks out her jaw menacingly. Her shoulders drop into attack posture.

"Okay. I'll take some agave in the strawberry lemonade."

"Same," Dick says.

The waitress walks away, muttering to herself. Skinny people can be amazingly feisty. My theory is that they're starving, that's why they're always in combat mode.

Dick doesn't seem interested in the menu, so I put mine on my lap. There's no room on the tiny table for food even.

"So," I say, "Can you please tell me what is so urgent that you have to meet me for lunch in the land of the tofu people?"

Dick laughs. "Swanson, you're so funny."

I frown. Dick has never given me credit for any positive attribute: humor, intelligence, professionalism. We definitely never meet for lunch or even a cup of coffee, which is kind of odd considering how closely we work together. Well, part of that is that I prefer bagels with cream cheese, while Dick thinks celery sticks and green tea is a gourmet treat, but nonetheless. Plus, he seems so happy today, definitely not like Dick either. Then, the fog of confusion suddenly lifts and I see what's happening. I blurt out, "You're in love!"

Devil Dog barks.

I wait for Dick to look abashed but he just grins. I know that grin. I used to grin like that.

"Her name is Clarisse Barnum. She's smart and funny and beautiful. And unexpected. I never met a woman who could surprise me like she does. Do you know how refreshing that is? I met her in a Bikram yoga class in Cambridge. "

"Naturally."

"And she has her life in order." He sighs. "It's such a relief to be around someone who knows where she put her car keys."

"Congratulations, Dick."

"Is that all you can say?"

"I'm sure you'll be very happy." Although the truth is, I can't imagine Dick being happy in anything as messy and unpredictable as love.

"Don't be snarky. It affects you, too, Swanson."

I fiddle with the end of the menu. "Your love life affects me *how?*"

Dick smooths down his hair. "Clarisse needs a divorce, Swanson. I told her I would help her."

"How are you going to help her?"

"By referring her to you of course."

"Of course."

"Swanson," he leans in to me. "I think she's the one."

"What do you mean, *the one?*"

"I want to marry her, Swanson."

"*Married?* I thought you were a confirmed bachelor."

"Funny, I thought so too."

"But you just met her!"

"I'm certain, Swanson. She has everything I ever wanted in a life partner."

I open the menu so he can't see my face. I don't want to admit that I depend on Dick for human companionship, as spotty and unsatisfying as his companionship is. But that's the truth. If he marries this Clarisse person, there's no telling where she will take him. That's the way marriages are. Two people join together and become a third persona that might decide it wants to live in *Spain* for god's sake and learn Flamenco dancing. Or become Pennsylvania Amish, or Kansas whatever-they-are. That's what so sad about the divorces I handle. It's like someone dies and instead of mourning, everyone spits on his grave.

"So, you'll represent her?" he asks. "In her divorce? I told her you were the best."

I slide the menu behind my back. I'm not hungry anymore and it's not just because I find Tagine of Green Bean unpromising. "Of course, I will, Dick. Congratulations. Really, I mean it. Tell her to come by my office and we'll start the paperwork."

He hands me a stuffed folder. "It's all in here. Except for the financial disclosures. You'll have to get that from her."

"Oh." Naturally Dick would have all the paperwork done.

"I got most of the forms off the net." He looks pleased with himself, for having finally plugged into the worldwide web—only about ten years after everybody else did. He has a cell phone now too.

"Look, Dick, I have to run. I have a one o'clock appointment, so…" I get up and yank Devil Dog.

"I think everything you need is in the file, but I'll call you tomorrow," Dick says. He is already buried in the world of bean sprouts and cruelty-free broccoli. And love. Let's not forget love. I can't.

Chapter 2

Do You Know How Hard It Is To Run In High Heels?

I flee the Holy Bean, hop in my Miata convertible which I had double parked on Charles Street in front of the beanerie with the emergency lights flashing, and cheer that I hadn't gotten a ticket. After I tie his leash to the door handle, Devil Dog swaggers on the back seat, going from one side to the other to bark. I peer into the side view mirror all ready to zoom off to find a hamburger joint when I see a meter maid coming up the sidewalk. She taps on my door. I pull my sunglasses down my nose to look at her, respectfully. You don't screw around with meter maids in Boston. In terms of power and influence, they are right up there with Whitey Bulger. They control The Boot.

She rests her hands on the door handle, looks up and down the Miata, casting a not-so-friendly look at Devil Dog and at the permit I had tossed on the dashboard before going into the restaurant. "You from the Congolese Embassy?" she asks. "Really?"

"Yes, I am, ma'm." I have a glove compartment full of phony permits that I put out when I am parked illegally, which I'm sorry, is just about everywhere in Boston. There isn't a single legal parking space in a toney neighborhood you don't have to pay a monthly fee for, so what's a working girl with a lot of appointments and places to be to do? I could park in the Commons Garage, but seriously? It's tortuous to hike in Jimmy Choo heels. So I use counterfeit parking permits. What would you do? No brainer, right? "Well, I'm not actually employed by the

Congolese Embassy, but I am doing business with them. The ambassador wants to divorce one of his wives. He gave me this," I hold up the permit that proclaims I am traveling on official Congolese business then quickly ditch it in the glove compartment, "I expedite things. When people want out of a divorce, they want out fast." I shake my head meaningfully.

"Tell me about it," she says and closes her ticket issuing folder. "That's what you do? Divorce?"

"Technically family law, but yeah." I hand her a card which she reads before slipping it into her pants pocket.

"You give discounts to civil servants?" she asks.

"No."

Her face falls.

"Yes. Okay. Call me for an appointment."

She smiles and I take off. See, this is why I am still making payments on my Miata and can't afford a secretary even though I've been in business for four years. I am a sucker for a fellow working woman who needs help. Maybe I should try representing men in divorces.

Traffic is horrible. I have to drive through the Boston University campus on my way to Brookline and the students are just returning from summer vacation. U-Hauls, Budget Rent-a-Vans and cars crammed with laptops, lacrosse sticks, and teddy bears are double parked the whole way in, with students greeting each other in the middle of the narrow campus lane, ignoring the traffic jams they're causing. I downshift and wait for a young woman in halter top and urban guerilla hot pants to finish holding court to a group of admirers who've left their cars idling to greet her, but Devil Dog gets impatient and starts barking at them. The princess notices and comes over to the car. "Hi honey," she squeals to Devil Dog who immediately gives in to her adoration. "God, I miss my dog," she says to me. "You're so lucky."

"You have plenty of admirers."

"It's not the same, is it?" she says looking back at her milling swain.

"No, it isn't." We exchange smiles, sisters under our very different skins.

The clump of cars finally moves when the princess retreats into her apartment turning for a final wave to her admirers as well as me and Devil Dog and before long we are speeding through Kenmore Square to Cleveland Circle and my office, stopping only once for the Green Line train to turn in front of us.

My office is in an old arcade building right off of Cleveland Circle. Most of the stores on the first floor have changed hands since I've moved in, but a couple are still run by ancient merchants and it makes me feel connected and safe that some things remain the same. The hosiery store is still run by a Hasid who tilts on the back legs of a kitchen chair outside the front door, his hairy arms locked over his enormous belly. When I pass, his usual greeting is "Zaftig, Zaftig!" Dick explained the subtleties of what that meant. He isn't there today and his shop is closed. Maybe, I think, it's a Jewish holiday. They always come at the end of summer. I feel a pang of disappointment not to hear him declare me ripe fruit in his booming voice and funny accent. I didn't know I was addicted.

I could take the rickety old elevator to the second floor, but inspired by the tofu people I decide to walk. I can make one flight at least in my Jimmy Choos and god knows, Devil Dog can use the exercise. Is there anything more pathetic than a Dachshund with its stomach dragging on the floor? When I finally make the landing, I'm huffing and when I squint in the dim light, I see a woman—back-lit—sitting outside my door. A walk-in! I cheer silently. I need two more new clients this month to replenish my secretary fund which I constantly raid to buy Jimmy Choos.

Devil Dog and I practically run down the hall to greet her and when she sees us she rises. The afternoon sun comes in through a window and hits her blond curls from behind, splintering the light into a thousand strands, making a kind of halo around her. I gasp.

She puts out her hand and I am thrown back to some primal religious memory, that's how ethereal she looks. I am dumbstruck and she gets sick of waiting for me to introduce myself. "You must be Swanson," she says. "I'm Clarisse Barnum."

When I continue gaping at her, she says, "Dick…"

"I know who you are," I say. "Come in."

Chapter 3

Meet The Girlfriend

When I get over my awe at Clarisse's beauty, we go into my office and I sit with the light behind my head, wondering if the sun is producing the same effect as it did behind Clarisse's head, but as Clarisse's eyes are businesslike my guess is no.

"Did Dick…" she says.

"He gave me this." I hold up the folder Dick gave me in the restaurant.

She sits back in her chair, relieved. "I want to get this over with as quickly as possible."

"That's what everyone says when they want a divorce."

"Do they? Well, when it's over, it's over, I guess. No use prolonging the misery."

"Dick is very fond of you," I say.

She looks blank for a minute. "Yes, of course. Dear Dick." She smiles. "I'm very fond of him, too."

When the sun is directly on her face, the magical effect subsides and she only looks like an ordinary gorgeous fashion model: about thirty years old with curly blond hair pulled back loosely in a long braid. No makeup needed to accentuate huge blue eyes. She seems pleasant enough, to be fair, although I am in no mind to be fair to the woman who wants to take away my one morsel of human companionship. But is that her fault? No. She looks a lot healthier than the women I saw in the Holy Bean, by that I mean she's got a shape and looks like she eats meat.

"Have you known Dick a long time? I've known Dick a long time, but the truth is I don't really know him well, you know?" I say.

"Dick? He is a rather private person, I know what you mean.

And he certainly has his peccadilloes."

She laughs into her hand and she peers at me to see what effect she is having on me. I feel a chill go up my spine. I don't trust her.

"He's very healthy," I say. "He keeps himself in tip top shape."

"I know! All that yoga, and measuring everything he eats."

She titters and I think that someone in love would find their beloved's eccentricity endearing. I pull her divorce papers out of the folder and read. Her soon-to-be ex-husband is Michel Meriodoc. The name sounds familiar.

"Meriodoc?" I say. "Is that French?"

"Yes!" Her expression brightens. "Do you know him?"

"Should I?"

"He is head of the French Farmer's Association. He makes sure that French agriculture stays au terroir, as they put it. I'm sure you've heard of him. He is a very important man."

"Maybe in France."

"No, no. Here too. He is fighting the importation of Frankenfood to France from the U.S."

"Frankenfood?"

"You know, genetically engineered food. Like frog genes in spinach. Like spinach genes in oranges. Frankenfood."

With all the other stuff to worry about with food—fat content, carbs, corn syrup, sodium, nitrates, salmonella—genetically engineered food doesn't make my list of things to worry about. "Why is he fighting that?"

"Because French people don't want to eat genetically modified food."

"Why? Is it bad for you?"

"Of course it's bad for you."

I nod and pretend to keep reading. Why was I getting the feeling that she was still in love with Meriodoc? Or at least not in love with Dick. But the image of Dick In Love kept coming up. He couldn't be so deluded as to be in love with a woman who— for whatever reason—was using him. And Dick was definitely in love. I suddenly knew what the term "blinded by love" meant.

"I have two uncles in France right now," I say.

"No kidding."

"No kidding. They went to the Cordon Bleu cooking school and now they want to open an American restaurant in Paris."

"For god's sake, no!"

"For god's sake, yes. Le Haut Dog. That's what they want to call it."

She shakes her head dismissively and sighs. "Do you have everything you need in there to process my divorce?"

I flipped through the paperwork. "No children?"

"No. Ah, of course, Michel has a son, grown, Sébastien. He'll inherit from his father no matter what happens in our divorce."

"Pre-nup?"

"No. We were in love. When you're in love you can't believe it will ever end." She smiles and shrugs. "But sometimes it does. Anyway, France has very old-fashioned inheritance laws, so we want the divorce done here. Dick didn't seem to think it would be a problem."

"You know Dick is a private investigator, don't you? He's not a lawyer."

"He said you're a very good attorney. Very sensitive to women's issues."

"Right."

"No, he really said that."

"Where are you from?" I ask, flipping through her paperwork. "Nebraska?" I look at the sophisticated woman in front of me trying to see her in overalls at a county fair. Not there. Well, when I go to lawyer conferences people always think I live next door to the Kennedys because I live in Massachusetts. Their minds just can't entertain the possibility of a Southie female attorney. So much for preconceptions. "Was your father a doctor or something?"

"I'll tell you about it sometime," Clarisse says and gives me her first genuine smile. She gathers up her tote. "Do you have everything you need? Are we done here?"

"Yes, I'll just look everything over and start the filing. Oh, now wait. I need your financial disclosure forms. I don't see them here."

"I almost forgot." She pulls out a sealed manila envelope and hands it to me. "I want us to be friends, Swanson," she says. "You know, any friend of Dick's I want to be a friend of mine."

She seems sincere. Maybe I was wrong to be suspicious. Although, if she was really close to Dick she would know Dick and

I weren't actually friends. Is that what he said we were? Maybe I'm getting paranoid. Maybe I just need a vacation. Maybe my uncles are right and I should visit them in France.

"I'll call you about next steps," I say. The red light on my cell phone starts to blink with incoming. I wave Clarisse out the door and say hello to Uncle Joe.

Chapter 4

I Wish, Sometimes, That Everyone Would Just Stay In One Place

"Uncle Joe!" I cry into the phone. And then I start crying. God, am I pathetic. Devil Dog rouses himself at the sound of my sobbing and sniffs the air.

"Swanson! Good news!" he says. "We found a location for Le Haut Dog! Right in Paris!"

I feel a heavy weight on my chest. It's official: they're never coming home. "That's just wonderful," I manage to croak.

"It's right in the 20th *arrondissemont.* Lots of foot traffic. Very diverse neighborhood. Lots of tourists."

I can hear a peculiar European sounding siren in the background. *Too doo too doo.*

"Just too *too* wonderful." God, how many times do I have to exclaim my fake enthusiasm?

"We got a couple of backers. Some wannabe cowboys from New York City. They love the idea of good old American food right smack in the middle of Paris. They say they can never find anything to eat here."

"I'll bet," I say, remembering Clarisse's disdain at the thought of American food. And she was only French by association. I pictured the headlines: Le Haut Dog With Secret Swanson Sauce Storms the Barricades of Paris! Yup, I bet the French just can't wait.

"But to make it really authentic, we want a diner."

"You want dinner?"

"No, no, no! A diner. One of those chrome things that look like train cars.

"Oh, a diner. Like the South Street Diner?"

"That's the one. Can you help us find one?"

"In Paris?"

"No! Find it there, in America, and our backers will buy it and ship it over here."

I blink a couple of times. The whole enterprise seems overwhelming. "You can do that? Ship a whole building?"

"You can do anything if you have enough money. And these guys have more than enough."

"I don't know how to do that," I whine.

"Look, we have the name of someone. Start with him and go from there. Got a pencil?"

I'm really sorry that phone connections have gotten so good. I loved the days where you could crackle a piece of paper into the mouthpiece of a phone and claim "bad connection, sorry!" and hang up. "Okay, shoot," I say.

Uncle Joe spells the name out for me—Guy de Guy—and gives me his phone number and email address. "He knows everyone!" he says. "He's a personcenti. That's a new word, Swanson. Like it?"

Uncle Joe is always coining new words and sending them to Merriam Webster at "no charge." I don't think they ever used one of his suggestions, but it doesn't dampen his enthusiasm.

"What do I call him? By his first name or last?" I ask. "Guy? Or Guy?"

"What?"

"Never mind. I was just trying to be funny." Tears run down my face. My uncles are never coming home and now they want my help in making sure they stay in Paris. I mean, once they move a whole building there, that's kind of permanent.

"This is going to be so much fun, Swanson," Uncle Joe says. "We're working on the menu now. You're going to love it. It's going to be a home away from home."

"What's wrong with the original home?" I ask. "Why do you need to go away from home to find another home? And why do you need a diner? Why don't you just open a chic eaterie like everyone else?"

"Swanson?" Uncle Stevie has grabbed the phone. "You okay, kid?"

"I'm fine." Of course, as soon as someone pities me I start to cry full force. I blow my nose loudly.

"Hey, hey. What's the matter? Was the trial awful?"

"Not too."

But of course it was awful. A nightmare. The trial was for Hidalgo's murderer, Ines, who just happened to be his sister who was aiming at me and missed, but hit her brother. She got manslaughter for that, but first degree for her murder of Carlton and Stone Bledsoe. I wasn't allowed to leave Boston until her trial was over. Now that it was, I felt like I was wearing cement shoes, unable to move on. "Yes, really awful."

"I knew it! You should take a vacation and come here immediately. You're just dwelling on it. You always dwell on things. Maybe you can combine a vacation with finding us a diner."

"I don't know why you need a diner. Anyway, I don't know if I can…"

"Thank you so much, Swanson! You don't know how much this means to us!"

And they click off. I put Guy de Guy's contact information in my purse and pull out a Reese's candy bar twin set—"give one to a friend!" the package says—and eat both because I don't have a friend, before putting some files in my briefcase. I go down the stairs and out on the street intending to walk home, but get back in my car instead.

Chapter 5

If Your Home Is Now A Hole In The Ground, Is That Still Your Home?

Every night after work for the last month, since the murder trial was over, I drive over to Southie to look at the holes in the ground that contain my memories. The hole in the ground that used to be the home where my uncles raised me. The other hole in the ground that used to be Mikey's Garage where I first met Hidalgo, bending over my BMW engine checking for imaginary flaws so we could talk until we both finally got the nerve to acknowledge our mutual attraction. There's nothing there yet as the entire construction project is tied up in lawsuits over the polluted mess they found underground and Native American claims of sacred burial grounds. Oh, yeah, and a Dunkin Donuts which refuses to acknowledge eminent domain and rises up among the stone and ashes like a pink Taj Mahal, sloppy stucco covering up the now lost original shapes of the hodgepodge group of buildings that make up the donut shop and living quarters of Dr. Saad and his family. The sweet smell of donuts and coffee still wafts over the landscape, but the hammer of the law is inevitable. Before construction starts they'll have to move like everyone else.

On the edge of the site which is like a set from Road Warrior is a yoga studio. Devil Dog and I get out of the car and walk nonchalantly past the glass storefront and look into the candle lit space like we've done every night. Everyone inside looks so peaceful and flexible. I always mean to go in and try it—yoga would give me a better excuse than nostalgia for coming back here—but I don't own tight black stretch pants and a tie-dyed tank top, which I keep meaning to buy but never find time to and anyway the sales clerk in LuluLemon pissed me off because she said she didn't think yoga clothes came in sizes larger than 10. Dick does yoga all the time. He swears by it. Claims he gets so much done because he's focused. But everyone in there looks so damn skinny, it's depressing.

The yoga instructor must feel my eyes on her back because she turns around, her hands in prayer-position over her chest, and smiles before surreptitiously giving me the finger while her class is in down-dog.

Dejected, I walk on to the Dunkin Donuts where I am greeted by the owner, Dr. Saad, who immediately brings a plate of chocolate covered donuts and a coffee with extra cream and sugar to a table by the window.

"Swanson! I was hoping you would come by this evening. Sit down, sit down!" and he shoos away his wife and daughters who are hovering behind me like bobbleheads—which I keep meaning to talk to them about, if they're going to be real American women they have to stop that—and pulls out a chair for me and points to the floor, "For the dog, for the dog" and one of his daughters brings out two bowls, one with water and one with a plain donut for Devil Dog. "I have good news. The city has finally come up with a price that is reasonable."

By which, I'm pretty sure, means it was outrageous. "I thought you weren't selling on principle."

"Yes. It was the price. Insulting. But now…"

"So this is it? You're selling?" Now I would have no place to go and remember my past. Where would I wear my cement shoes? "How much?"

He leaned in and whispered a number in my ear, then sat back. "For this?"

"What's wrong with this? This is my life! They want to buy my life? They have to pay." He crosses his arms and looks at his wife and daughters who are looking on anxiously. "They want to go to college. They're like you. They don't want husbands. They want careers. So." He shrugs. "Talk to them about how happy you are. Go ahead."

"I was about to get married, you know."

"I know. Now it's too late. You are too old."

He laughs.

"Only kidding. But they want to go to college. What can I do? It's not cheap."

"No, it's not cheap."

It was late August and the days already had that autumn tang which always makes me sad and they were definitely getting shorter. I was facing the setting sun and if I squinted I could almost make out in the rubble the neighborhood I grew up in. When this building was gone, there would be nothing left of my past. I'm thirty years old and haven't even lived most of life yet and I'm mooning over my past? I know. It's weird. I'm the young person. I'm supposed to be moving on. Maybe I was meant to be one of those curios people visit when they bring their grandchildren to show them where they grew up. "That old lady on the stoop. That's Swanson Herbinko. I had a crush on her in kindergarten."

"Well, this is just great!" I say, and raise my paper cup to Dr. Saad who is delighted with my good wishes.

The bell at the entrance jingles and I turn to see Dick coming through the door.

"Dick! What are you…" I ridiculously think he had been in the yoga studio, but as far as I know he never comes to Southie.

"Swanson, I knew I would find you here."

He looks pale and I stand up and grab his arm because it seems as if he might keel over.

"What! What?"

"Michel Meriodoc has been murdered."

"Michel Meriodoc?" I say, then remember as Dick and I say it at the same time, "Clarisse's husband."

Chapter 6

When Is A Wife A Murder Suspect?

It's the first time since I met him, that Dick seems incapable of action. He allows me to put my arm around him and walk him to my car then drives back with me to my apartment in Brookline where he asks me to book flights to Paris for him and Clarisse online.

"Where is she anyway?" I ask, punching one-way information Boston to Paris into Expedia.

"Back in Cambridge. Packing."

"She probably shouldn't go back. She's the wife. She's the prime suspect."

"Don't be ridiculous. She already filed for divorce. Didn't you file those papers yet?"

"Dick, I only got them this afternoon."

"Plus, she was here." He stretches his mouth into a fake smile like a sad clown.

"You can always hire someone to do your dirty work," I say. "I hear France has a high unemployment rate."

"She won't get anything if she deserts him. And if she doesn't go back, she deserted him. And anyway French inheritance laws are completely different than ours. I haven't gotten around to studying them yet. That was going to be your job."

"Right. Well, here you are." I point to the screen that has two flights out of Boston tomorrow. "Which one do you want?"

"Let me ask Clarisse." He phones her and while I hear only one side of their conversation, something seems wrong. Psst, psst, whisper, whisper. I initially thought that Clarisse still loved her husband, but now I'm thinking that maybe she killed the guy. Maybe I'm just jealous of her. Jealous of someone perfect enough to catch the attention of someone like Dick, someone who has every aspect of their life nailed down. I don't have any systems in place, no routines to make my life more efficient. If Devil Dog wasn't extremely vocal about his needs, I would probably forget to walk him.

After a lot more murmuring, Dick comes back in the room seeming a lot more composed and says, "Book us the ten o'clock."

I hold out my hand. "Credit card. Passport numbers."

He looks at me blankly.

"You don't expect me…? Okay, but it's against future earnings." There goes my next pair of Jimmy Choos. As well as my secretary. Not to mention the car payment on the Miata. I would have to trade it in for a used Honda. "I don't have your passport numbers," which he pulls up on his iPhone. Of course. I'm not sure where my passport is. Do I even have one?

"Two tickets at 900 dollars each, that's 1,800 dollars," I say peevishly. "It's the airport fees that'll kill you."

"Two tickets? Aren't you coming with us?"

"Why should I come with you?"

"Swanson, you have to come with us."

"I have work to do. Work here."

"What cases are you working on?"

I don't have to think hard. The only case I was working on was Clarisse's divorce. And that was obviously superseded by murderous events.

"Yessssss. I have some irons in the fire."

"Really?"

"I have to find my uncles a diner." I tell him about their request.

"Well, get that going and come over."

"Excuse me, Dick, but why do I have to go to France? Give me one good reason."

"There's been a murder and my future wife is involved up to her neck."

"I'm not a criminal lawyer, Dick, I'm a divorce lawyer. It appears that Clarisse no longer needs a divorce and frankly, I'm way out of my league here."

"You don't have to be an expert in criminal law to figure things out. My gut is telling me this murder is political and I need someone with a good head on her shoulders to help me figure things out."

Good head on her shoulders? Am I hearing this right?

"But it's France! I don't even speak French."

"Don't make me say it, Swanson."

"What? You think I can't survive here without you? That's it, isn't it?"

"Is that what you think?"

Actually, it is.

Dick laughs. "It's funny how we're never sure what other people think of us, isn't it? To be perfectly honest, Swanson, the only reason I want you to come is because they're probably going to gang up on Clarisse and I want you on our team."

Chapter 7

Technically Speaking, Backwards Isn't A Direction

See how easy I am? Dick and Clarisse need me on their team so I set my alarm clock so I would be up in time to take them to the airport as well as do the million other things I needed to do, like find a diner.

At eight o'clock I'm seated at the counter at Max's Deli on Beacon Street, ordering an everything bagel with lox and cream cheese and enjoying the best coffee in Brookline. And looking at the Boston Globe international news headlines on my iPhone. Michel Meriodoc's murder is very big news. No suspect yet. But a ceramic owl, symbol of the Athena Corporation, was found by his head. A link sends me to another article on Athena, dated a month ago, and I get why Dick says Michel Meriodoc's murder may have been political. Athena is the biggest food importer in France and they've been pushing to have GMO products allowed into France. Clarisse's husband was their most influential opponent.

"You're here early, Swanson," Max says, mopping up the counter.

"I got stuff to do, before I go to France." I say it nonchalantly and am inordinately pleased at how sophisticated it makes me sound, even if last week I would have sneered at anything to do with France.

"France? No kidding."

"I've got to get a passport." Turns out I don't have one. And why should I? I've never been anywhere. "And buy a ticket to Paris. And find a diner."

"What do you mean, 'find a diner'? What's the matter with here?" Max looks hurt.

"Not to eat at. To buy. The building. For my uncles. They're opening a restaurant in Paris and they want an old American diner to put it in."

"Americans are crazy, you know that?" Max says. "Why would they want to ship a diner to Paris when everyone here is tearing them down?"

"I don't know. Uncle Joe says they're hip."

"Hip!" Max almost wears a hole in the counter, rubbing in a circle in one area. "Hip!"

"I'm not hip either, Max," I say.

"I'm very hip," Max says, menacing me with his rag. "I'm like on the other side of hip. Reverse hip is even hipper than being hip. I'm anti-hip."

Max is wearing brown check polyester pants and a blue drip-dry shirt. He alternates this outfit with a pair of black polyester pants and blue drip-dry shirt. Connie, his wife, does the wash every other day and he's been on this rotation ever since I've been coming here. It does seem sort of hip. Leaving a small carbon footprint of polyester.

"What kind of food are they going to serve?" he asks.

"I dunno. American? The place is going to be in an American diner and be called Le Haut Dog. Probably eggs and toast and burgers. But who knows? I sure don't."

"Le Haut Dog, eh? That's very good. I would go to Paris, too, except, you know." He gestures with his head towards the kitchen where Connie is slicing tomatoes and pickles for the lunch rush. "She would never go for it."

Connie, who I swear has some kind of radar which detects when people are saying things she doesn't approve of, stabs the counter with her knife, which stands on end, and comes out with her arms crossed to stare at me. "Swanson," she says.

"Hi, Mrs. Oppenheimer."

"We're not leaving again," she says. "Certainly not to go back to Europe. That's going backwards. I keep telling him. Why would we want to go backwards?"

"You shouldn't go backwards," I say.

"Maybe not stay here," she looks around critically. "There are better places ahead of you, always, but never behind you. If it were up to me, they would get rid of rear view mirrors in cars. You know? The ones you look into to see what's behind you. I think that's a bad habit to get into."

I should point out the safety issues involved, but as Connie doesn't look like she wants a lecture, Max and I nod our heads in agreement and she goes back into the kitchen, picks up her knife and resumes her thwacking.

"I don't want my uncles to stay there, either," I say. "I don't know what they find so interesting in Paris that they can't find here."

Max snorts. "Are you kidding? Women! French women!"

The thwacking in the kitchen stops, and Max and I freeze, but soon the knife work resumes.

"You think my uncles like French women?" It hadn't occurred to me that women were keeping them there. But of course. Jeez, how stupid could I be?

"Well, in any event, I promised I would find them a diner and ship it over. Do you have any idea where I can find one of those?"

"A diner? No. They're tearing them down all over the place. The Greeks own all the diners now and they want them to look like ballrooms."

"Would you ask around for me?" I ask.

"Naturally."

He waves me away when I hand him a fiver. "No way, Swanson. Get out of here and go to France." My uncles loaned Max money when he first opened and he never lets me pay.

He winks and whispers, "Send me a French postcard."

I pinch his cheek. "I will."

Chapter 8

If You Loved Him So Much, Why Are You Divorcing Him?

Clarisse cries the whole way to the airport, softly, into a monogrammed handkerchief. It's not the way I cry and it's annoying. She just found out the gory details of Michel's murder, which is, granted, pretty shocking: a bullet in the chest, right to the heart while he was getting out of his car, a vintage Bentley, which he had just parked in his garage. A ceramic statue of an owl was on the passenger seat, which as I read in the paper is the symbol of the international food conglomerate Athena.

"Which is pushing their food and seeds everywhere," Dick says. "They can't stand it that France will not give them a stamp of approval, it won't even allow their products in the country. It was what Michel was fighting for."

"Don't you have some medication you can give her?" I whisper to Dick.

"She's in mourning. You don't want to block that," he says. "Her grief could surface in any part of her body and wreak havoc."

"Is that your theory or the medical profession's?" I ask.

"No difference."

I wasn't used to seeing so much emotion for an ex. Certainly not in my business where ex-spouses try to stomp each other into the ground. It was a level of sophistication I wasn't used to. I pull into the international departure terminal at Logan.

"He must have been quite a guy," I say sarcastically.

"He is. Was. He was one of those people who tried to do the

right thing. "

"It was only about food," I say. "It wasn't like stopping war."

"Only food? Swanson, you have so much to learn. He was a real hero."

Keeping France's spinach pure. Whatever.

"So, see you in a couple of days," I say, opening the trunk so they can get their suitcases out.

"Please, Swanson, don't dawdle."

Devil Dog barks good-bye and I drive off to the Federal Building to take care of my passport. I was told that morning on the phone, after being put on hold for 40 minutes, that I could request an emergency passport and be ready to go in 48 hours. Just enough time to take care of this diner business.

I fish around my purse and pull out Guy de Guy's phone number and dial while waiting to get into the Sumner Tunnel. No one ever answers their cell phones, so I'm surprised when a gravelly voice says, "Ah, *oui?*"

I clear my throat. "Mr. Guy?"

"*Oui.*"

"Do you speak English?"

"*Oui.*"

"Okay, *oui*. Well, my uncles, Steve and Joe Herbinko…"

"Ah, Steevee and Cho. How are they?"

"Yes, Steevee and Cho. They said I should contact you about a diner?"

"About dinner?"

"No, a diner. They want to buy a diner and ship it…" but before I can explain the whole thing yet again, Guy is telling me how to get to his apartment on Marlborough Street in the Back Bay and no, he doesn't mind dogs. "We can talk about the diner over dinner," he says.

I stop by a CVS to take care of my passport picture, drive to the Federal Building to drop off my emergency passport application and then drive across town to the Back Bay. It's not a date or anything, but for some reason my neck is tingling. Even Devil Dog is revved, running from one side of the back seat to the other. I reach back to pet him and he licks my hand. I am so grateful to have Devil Dog. During Hidalgo's murder trial he listened to me cry every night, nudging me awake with his leash between his teeth to walk him when I fell asleep in front of the television in the living room with the lights on. Whining when I forgot to put out food for him, which reminded me to put out food for myself. Or at least call out for some. Making me laugh by doing something cute when I was paralyzed with grief and thinking there was no reason to get out of the chair.

The dinner invitation from Guy de Guy feels like someone opened a door and let some light in and I don't close my eyes against it.

"You know what, Devil Dog? We're going to be all right, boy. I think we're going to be all right."

Chapter 9

What Is A Lifestyle Critic, Anyway?

Guy's apartment is right across the street from the French Library, which I guess shouldn't be surprising. What is surprising is that I find a parking space right in front of the private school on the corner. The sign specifically says you can't park there during school hours and, hooray! School is out for the day. I feel my life may be improving for the better since I've decided to crack out of my gloom and help my uncles get their diner and help Dick solve the Meriodoc's murder so he has clear sailing with Clarisse.

I see a whole life where the world is opening doors for me because I'm doing good for my fellow women and men. I find number 72, ring the bell for apartment three, and after three bolts slam open, the door itself finally follows suit and there is Guy. He is a slight man, about 30, with chin-length dark blond hair and a soul patch under his lip which is full and sensuous. I find myself looking at that lip a couple seconds longer than necessary—in case I have to identify it later, I tell myself—and when I look up at his eyes, I see that he is laughing at me.

"So you are the famous Swanson!" he says. "Named after a frozen dinner."

I nod. It sounds so awful when he says it. "Breaded chicken and mashed potatoes," I say.

"And this is the famous Deveel Dog!"

"*Oui*," I say. "Named after the famous Deveel Dog," which chocolate pastry treat Guy obviously never heard of, but Devil Dog stands at attention accepting Guy's admiration, something

Guy seems to understand.

"So I think," he says, pulling me into his apartment, "Why not have dinner, if we will do business together? Civilized, no?"

The apartment is the first floor of an old Back Bay mansion. Twelve foot high ceilings. Big marble fire place. Everything painted white. Books and CDs strewn all over the place. Paintings are propped against the wall, on top of shelves, and on the floor but none are hung.   It's a mess.

Something, though, smells very good.

"Duck stuffed with green olives," he says, even before I ask. "It will take a while to be done, but it was all I had."

I imagine what it would be like to try to rustle a dinner together for an unexpected guest. I don't even know what's in my freezer. The only reason a duck would be in my refrigerator is if it flew in there by mistake.

"Will you join me in a drink?" he asks, cracking the label on a new bottle of Laphroaig 10 which is sitting on a silver tray with two baccarat glasses and an ice bucket. He pours some Scotch over ice and hands me the glass. It seems odd that he didn't offer me a choice, but I decide that it's the way the French do things.

"I'm not really a drinker," I say, taking the glass.

"What do you mean you're not a drinker? Americans always say things like that. I don't drink, I don't smoke, I don't eat red meat, I don't eat cheese. You are so extreme. Who doesn't eat cheese? It's absurd. Cheese is one of life's pleasures. I don't understand how you can be so absolute about things and be happy." He sits down on a brown leather sofa and motions for me to sit next to him. "I don't bite, don't worry little girl," he laughs.

I know he's making fun of me, but for the first time since Hidalgo died I find myself interested in a man. This man. "I mean," I say, politely taking a sip, "that I don't drink too much."

"Too much. Of course not! Everything should be in moderation. Otherwise you become the thing you eat or do. Who wants to become a wheel of cheese, eh?"

He goes to the kitchenette which is against the back wall of exposed brick. It is open, but separated from the living room by a counter. Finally he comes back with a board of cheese and a long loaf of French bread. He tears off a piece of bread and smears it with soft cheese and hands it to me. "See this," he says, "Is part of the pleasure of life. Here, take it."

I daintily nibble on the end. It's very good. I find myself thinking of bagels with cream cheese and lox and I know those can't compete with the concoction this Frenchman just handed me. I take a long drink of the Scotch which is likewise great.

"We should talk about the diner," I say.

He waves his hand through the air. "We have plenty of time for that. An America diner in the 20th Arrondissement! Your uncles are a little crazy, no?"

I get red. But now I'm not sure if it's the Scotch or that my uncles were just insulted. "My uncles are not crazy. I thought you were their friend."

"Don't be angry with me. I want to sell your uncles a diner. Believe me! But they are visionaries and visionaries are a little crazy. There's nothing wrong with that. I am crazy also. Maybe, you are not crazy. Maybe you are an ordinary person, not crazy at all, very ordinary."

He sits down on the leather chair across from me and throws a leg over the arm while he watches this pronouncement sink in.

"I've had a couple of crazy moments in my life," I say.

"I'm sure you have done crazy very original things," he says. "Sorority girl pranks. Taking off your underwear and selling it to frat boys. Stealing the dean's, how do you call it, scepter? Very original."

I'm embarrassed, because that's exactly what I did when I was pledging Pad Thai Woo at Tufts. It seemed incredibly original and daring at the time, but now I can see it was ridiculous. I think that's what I always hated about the French, although I never thought about it until right this moment. They think that innocent hijinks are unsophisticated, while IMHO they are just a crabby culture that finds it terribly original to just criticize other people's fun instead making up their own.

"I don't understand how you can have such definite opinions about things," I say, emboldened by the Scotch. "How can you be so sure that you're right about everything?"

"Are you kidding? It's my job to be right about everything. To have definite opinions about everything."

"What exactly is your job? Are you like some kind of broker?"

"You mean the diner? Bowf. I just do that on the side. I am

the writer of Critic's Choice."

"Never heard of it."

"See you have opinions too. By saying that you imply that it isn't important. You haven't heard of it. Yet, anyone with sophisticated taste subscribes to my blog. It is the most influential publication of its kind in France. Well, other parts of Europe, too."

I put my glass out and Guy refills it. "So, what's it about?"

"Lifestyle."

"You're a lifestyle critic?" I laugh. "Your place is a mess."

"I didn't say housekeeping critic. I said lifestyle."

And here I have to admit, I don't know what he's talking about.

"Americans. You don't really have lifestyles. You have barbeques and take-out and LL Bean. It's as if you're living on the lam, waiting to go somewhere else. All your outdoor gear in the trunk of your car. Kayaks tied to the roof as if you have to make a quick getaway. And guns. What do you need all those guns for?"

"French have guns, too. Michel Meriodoc was shot, with a gun, obviously."

"I'm surprised you heard about that," he says. "Although it's a very big deal in France."

He looks at me with what I believe is new respect.

"I am somewhat personally involved as well." I tell him about Dick and Clarisse.

"You know Clarisse Barnum?" Now he is genuinely impressed if slightly incredulous as I tell him how my private investigator is in love with her and wants my help finding Meriodoc's murderer so Clarisse can be cleared for take-off.

But then it was my turn to be impressed when I tasted the duck stuffed with olives which was done a half-hour and three drinks later. "This is the most incredible poultry I ever had," I tell him in awe.

"I know." He smiles next to me at the kitchen counter where we're sitting on wicker stools.

"I don't know how people can be vegans, or even vegetarians," I say. "In fact..."

"I know!" he says, patting my thigh and I feel myself blush all the way down to my knee.

Devil Dog who has been sleeping by my feet, nips my toe,

which I had liberated from its Jimmy Choo while I was still on the sofa. I know Devil Dog is chastising me, but I offer him a piece of duck which mollifies him.

Then a salad with a simple lemon and oil dressing with a little parsley and then Guy passes the cheese board around again. All the while we are drinking wines which are coordinated with the food. I never understood how people could do that, remember flavors in their mind and imagine what will go with what. It seems to be an art. That's what my uncles are doing now, I think. They're dreaming up a new restaurant and menu. I am very happy for them that they are able to make people happy with their art.

"What about the diner?" I ask suddenly.

"Don't worry about it. I will totally take care of your uncles. I actually think I know where one is. People are always asking for them."

"You mean you've done this before?"

"Diners are nostalgia and there is always a market for nostalgia. I, however, am totally against nostalgia. What is the point in looking back when life is in front of you, staring you right in the face?"

I can't be sure if it's the booze, but I am feeling quite warm and cozy and not nostalgic in the least. Guy sets a fire in the fire place which takes the chill off the late summer night which is pouring into the apartment because both huge windows in the living room are wide open with no screens, "the better," he says, "to see the night sky. Even in the city, you can see the sky if you try." Devil Dog settles down in front of the fire. Guy and I argue about American culture, "an oxymoron" he pronounces, French food—which hornet's nest, he says, I will be stepping right into when I start poking around Michel Meriodoc's murder. We have cognac—a must after dinner, he insists—then he brews us coffee in a French press, and when I finally feel like I've sobered up enough to drive and say I have to leave, Guy leans over and kisses me.

"Merci, mademoiselle Swan, for a very pleasant evening."

I smile. I gather Devil Dog in my arms and carry him down the brownstone stairs to my car. I pass a couple strolling home from a party or perhaps dinner in town and we nod at one another and I don't feel so awfully alone because five minutes before I was part of a couple too. It felt nice. When I get in the car—which by the way, has a ticket on it, but I'm in such a good mood I don't care about the ticket—I think, did Guy call me Swan or did I just not hear him right because of the Cognac? Whatever. I don't look into the rear view mirror as I pull out.

Chapter 10

Dog Days

Despite assurances that my passport will be delivered the next day, it is not, and my anxiety is compounded by having to deduce what I need to do to make Devil Dog into a Frenchman. A micro-chip for starters, although Uncle Stevie told me they put one in when the vet fixed him. But apparently, after much searching on the net, it's not the right size micro-chip. The French want a 15 line chip and Americans only use a 9 line chip, so I'll have to bring my own bar code scanner. Plus I have to get two health certificates for him as well as a rabies shot.

"Jeez," I tell the vet, "You'd think they didn't have dogs in France, they're so paranoid about germs."

"They have their own germs to worry about," Ashley, Devil Dog's vet tells me. "They don't need ours too."

I wonder if Ashley is a secret Francophile and if I should hold that against her. She fills out all the paperwork and hands it to me. "Devil Dog is very healthy. Are you still feeding him Organic Dog?"

Organic Dog is the brand of kibble she gave me when I first brought Devil Dog in for a check-up. Devil Dog hated it and I worried he was going to starve to death so I started giving him a little of whatever I was eating.

"I'm so jealous of you going to France."

"Really?"

"I went there right after college. It was the best time I ever had in my life. Oh, here," she grabs a pen and writes something on her prescription pad and hands it to me. "It's the brand you should get in France."

Le Chien Vert. That'll happen. "Great, thanks so much, Ashley."

"It's so important to give him the right food. He's so short, that even a little extra weight will bog him down."

"Gotcha."

I pull Devil Dog out of the office and go to Petco to buy a carrier for him. He growls at all of them and I have to admit I'm not crazy about putting him in a cage for an entire transatlantic flight.

We finally settle on a carrier that's big enough for an Irish Wolf Hound and I let Devil Dog try it out on the backseat on the way home. I look at him in the rearview mirror.

"What do you think? Huh? It's like you're not even in a cage."

When I get home I read the rules and regulations again for animal travel on Air France and see that pet and carrier's weight must not exceed 6 kilograms, which is a little over 13 pounds so I take the carrier back and get a soft bag to carry Devil Dog.

By now it's four o'clock. I call the passport office again and they assure me it's been issued and it should arrive tomorrow in time for my flight which is ten o'clock out of Logan.

I go to Max's Deli to grab a bite. He's not there, but Connie is. She's cleaning up to close for the day.

"I can't make anything hot," she says.

I never figured out what I did to get on Connie's bad side—oh, now wait, I know. I made her take Howie Carr, the greyhound I rescued last summer and she's scared of dogs. She gave Howie back, which just goes to show that people never do what's good for them. A dog would have definitely improved her temperament. Anyway, she's short with me and always glares at Devil Dog as if he's about to bite her leg.

"I'll just have coffee," I say.

She puts down the mop. "I said nothing hot."

"Oh, I just thought it was already in the pot."

She points to the urn. "Clean."

"Okay. Never mind."

She grunts, and I pull Devil Dog towards the door. *The Boston Globe* is laying on the counter. I pick it up. "Mind if I take this?"

"Go ahead," she says and comes up behind me to lock the door.

t.   Michel Meriodoc's murder has been demoted to the inside of the first section. No suspects. How can they have no suspects? Wasn't that statue of an owl, the logo of the Athena corporation, found at the murder site, like a calling card? I suddenly want to be in France, helping Dick figure it out. But there's nothing I can do until tomorrow.

I'm at loose ends and I have—I look at my phone—more than 30 hours till my flight. I have an urge to call Guy de Guy, but that's silly. We just had one dinner and it wasn't even a date. Although it was a pretty spectacular dinner. Well, and that kiss wasn't bad either. Did all Frenchmen kiss you goodnight after a dinner date, I wonder? Maybe France wouldn't be so bad.

Devil Dog pulls me towards my car, which I left on the street instead of parking it in the garage. He thinks we're going to Southie to look at the hole. But I don't feel like it. It's just a hole, I tell myself. It isn't my life. My life is ahead of me.

"I think we should pack and go to bed early, Devil Dog," I say. "We have a long day ahead of us. And who knows what's coming after that."

Chapter 11

Is That A Gun, Lady, Or Is That Your Bra?

Devil Dog in tote, I make it to the airport just in time to crawl through security and board. Ashley had given me a couple of sedatives for Devil Dog and he is sound asleep in the cloth carrier on rollers that I am allowed to stow under the seat in front of me as long as he's knocked out. The security guard opens his carrier and checks him out, but he remains comatose. I give her all my papers—mostly in French which I'm sure she doesn't understand—but she surprises me by being Haitian and does. I think I'm home free, when naturally the underwires in my bra set off the metal detector and I endure the giantess security guard passing the wand over my boobs as if she were playing a video game. Bing, bing, bing!

"It's my bra," I say.

"No kidding. Why'd you wear a bra like that when you know you're going through a metal detector?" she asks me.

"It's the only kind of bra I have."

She takes me and Devil Dog to a side room where I have to take everything off and what seems like a roomful of security squashes my clothing with her hands looking for the offending piece of metal.

"It's my bra," I say.

After four guards conclude that it is my bra, I'm allowed to dress and Devil Dog and I are flying to our gate where everyone else has already boarded. Two airline employees, one talking on a walkie-talkie, are closing up shop and in the middle of closing the door when I run up to them.

"Wait! I'm on that flight!" I yell.

The woman flight attendant gives me a look of exasperation, checks my boarding pass and allows me in. I run down the passenger hallway to the airplane, not an easy thing in my new heels, which I bought just for this occasion, pulling Devil Dog in his rolling carrier, am greeted by a couple of flight attendants in French, Bonjour! although one recognizes me for what I am—an American—and says, "Hello. No room overhead, put you bag under the seat in front of you," when he realizes it's a dog. "Do you have all the paperwork?" he asks and when I assure I do, he says, "Good, because it's a nightmare getting into France if you don't."

And with that awful prophecy hanging over my head, I sidle down the aisle, looking for 25F, saying "Pardon, pardon!" to everyone whose elbow I was hitting, which was everyone's, until I finally see an empty aisle seat, look up to confirm it's 25F, shove Devil Dog under the seat in front of me, plop down and buckle up. I sigh. The man at the window seat turns to me and while I wrack my brain for a French phrase of greeting so the flight isn't too awkward, I see that the man is smiling at me. And I see that the man is Guy de Guy.

Chapter 12

My Head's In The Clouds

"Wha…..?"

"Amazing coincidence, no?" he says.

"I'll say."

"It's *ma soeur*. My sister. She is having man problems and needs my support."

"I'm sorry," I say.

"No, don't be sorry. I never liked him very much. She woke up yesterday morning with a black eye and decided she didn't like him either."

"Now I'm really sorry."

"But the good news is, I can see you. I was worried about that."

I was worried about that, too, but I never dreamed my dilemma would have such a fast solution.

"What about the diner?" I ask. "Not to take anything away from your sister, but…"

Guy holds up his hand. "No worries. I have one and it's on its way. I spoke with Uncle Cho this morning."

"Wow. You really work fast."

He smiles. The flight attendant comes down the aisle counting heads. I push Devil Dog's bag under the seat in front of me a little further so no one makes a big deal about having a dog on board until we take off.

"This is your first time in France, right?" he asks me.

"This is my first time anywhere," I say.

"You will definitely need a guide to help you navigate French society."

"I'm not going to be in society, exactly," I say. "My uncles are hot dog vendors from Southie and I don't think they've jumped too many rungs up the social ladder just because they attended the Cordon Bleu."

"But you are an *avocate*. A lawyer. That puts you on a different social level."

Maybe in France, I think.

Just to show Guy I can be all business despite how he is looking at me I pull out my file on Clarisse Barnum and start to read it. Dick had included a sealed envelope labeled "résumé" which I had ignored—I mean who cares where a divorcée went to school, right? I take it out of its envelope now and smooth it on my lap. It's a single-spaced letter addressed to me and written by Dick, which is curious. Across the top of the letter, he had handwritten: "I thought you should know who you are dealing with." Clarisse was the farm girl from Nebraska she claimed to be, it turns out. Her father, though, was a failure at farming. He could never bring a full crop to market until he discovered GMO soybeans—a could-not-fail-crop—in the late nineties, eventually becoming a salesman for the seeds. It turned out he was better suited to sales than farming.

Before that late success, though, when she was being raised in the flatlands her family lived in what they called a "foundation house," that is, in the foundation of a house that never got completely built. Tarps, plywood and old roofing materials kept them dry if not warm against the bitter blasts of winter. Most the money her father managed to make went into his Harley, which was named "Daddy's Dream" and which he displayed at motorcycle rallies in places like Sturgis, South Dakota—these rallies were like butch Mardi Gras, they pulled in thousands of attendees—in a vignette with Clarisse and her little sister, Mandy, in Harley tees, one sitting on daddy's bike, one pretending to service it. Under no circumstances, they were instructed, were they to talk to anyone, especially they were never to tell anyone their names or addresses because members of the Hell's Angels would scout these shows looking for people who were easy to strike up a conversation with, find out where they lived, and then come and steal the Harley, mostly, but other things of value as well. The

Angels had a big presence in the Midwest that was off the media's radar. They would also abduct women—go to road houses in the middle of nowhere, find out which waitresses had no one waiting for them and kidnap them after their shift. No one would file a missing persons' report, because there was no one to notice they were missing. Waitresses were easy prey. They moved around all the time, leaving the Midwest flatlands in winter for Texas or New Mexico, going back again in the summer. I'd probably never considered, Dick wrote, living in the cramped Northeast, just how vast and empty this country is.

Clarisse was one of these women. She'd exchanged the brutality of her parents' existence for the brutality of life on her own on the prairie and that, combined with her model good looks, made her a mark. She'd lived with an Angel "family" in Fargo, North Dakota for a year until the family was busted for having a meth lab in the basement of its headquarters. She'd managed to survive without getting pregnant and had bought herself status by becoming adept at cutting meth with baking soda and something called Vitabland that veterinarians use. While the skill wasn't a transferable vocation, the experience had taught her to think on her feet and find a way to profit from any situation she found herself in.

I put the letter down on my lap. "Holy Hannah!" I say aloud.

"Everything okay?" Guy asks, looking over my shoulder.

I cover the letter with the envelope of Clarisse's financial disclosures. "Fine. Look, we're taking off."

The flight attendant comes down the aisle and tells me to put my briefcase under the seat until we are cruising, which I do, and then I clutch the two armrests, my knuckles turning white as we quickly ascend into the clouds.

"It's the most dangerous part of the flight, the take-off and landing," Guy informs me.

He pats my hand and tries to extricate it from the armrest, but it doesn't budge. "Chère Swan," he says laughing. "I have something for your nerves."

When we are finally cruising, and the flight attendant is coming around with drinks, he orders us two double Scotches, "That's fine, no?" he asks as an afterthought. "And here." He taps two pills out of a brown prescription bottle. "This will help you sleep."

"Is that all they do?" I ask, examining the tiny pink pills.

"Yes, just sleep."

I pop them both with a long swig of Scotch and I must've zonked out because the next thing I know a flight attendant is walking down the aisle with a basket of hot washcloths which he distributes with a pair of tongs.

"Wash your face with it," Guy tells me when it's obvious I'm don't know what to do with it.

"Are we there, already?" I lean over him to look out the window. We are still over the ocean, but the Fasten Seat-Belt sign is on. "I can't believe I slept the whole way..." I suddenly remember Devil Dog. I pull him and his tote carrier out between my feet. He looks at me balefully through the mesh zippered cover and whimpers. His sedative must be wearing off, too. I push him back.

"Wow," I say. "I never sleep this soundly."

"You needed it," Guy says.

It's nice to have someone looking out for me again, I think. "So, where does your sister live?"

"Outside of Orleans."

"Ah." That means nothing to me.

"I will find you when I am finished with my sister."

"I don't know where I am going to be," I say. It seems a big waste to be in France and not have Guy as a guide.

"We know lots of people in common. Your uncles. France is, in a lot of ways, a very small country."

Guy walks Devil Dog and me to customs then glides through the European Union line and disappears from view. When I clear customs, Devil Dog and I are escorted to a private room with other Americans who are reuniting with drugged animals. Some of the pet owners are arguing in loud voices with the Animal Control officials. When it's our turn, the Animal Control officer takes one look at Devil Dog, smiles and says in good English, "A fierce breed. Fierce and handsome." He lifts Devil Dog out of his carrier. Devil Dog vogues for the officer. He stands perfectly erect and stares straight ahead in line with his now perpendicular tail. What a ham.

"This is one of the oldest breeds, you know," the officer says.

"How so?" I ask. I always thought the Dachshund breed was

an experiment gone awry and I assumed my uncles got me Devil Dog as a kind of hot dog joke.

"They were bred in the 1600s in Germany to find and kill badgers. They could go into burrows, find the badger, and fight it to the death."

Devil Dog turns his head and regards me with a definite "I was hoping you would find this out eventually" look then turns away with dignity.

"No kidding?"

The officer flips through my papers, makes me show him my bar code reader and how it works on Devil Dog's microchip, then stamps all the papers about a million times and we are free to go.

I put Devil Dog back in his carrier and carry him out of the office.

"I should have known," I tell Devil Dog. In our last adventure, he fought off a dominatrix, Ulrike Meiner, who was trying to kill me. Maybe Ulrike reminded him of a badger with her squinty blue eyes.

We walk to the double automatic doors which swing open, revealing a crowd of people behind a velvet rope who strain to see if we are the ones they are waiting for.

I put Devil Dog's carrier down and let him out, clipping on his leash. I scan the crush of people and see a pair of hands waving over everyone's heads.

"Swanson, Swanson! Over here!" Uncle Joe yells. He's pushing through the people, but Uncle Stevie gets there first, engulfs me in his big arms, picks me up and swings me around. Devil Dog, obviously fully recovered from his sedative, starts barking, but I don't care.

"We're here!" I shout. I almost say, "We're home," but I catch myself. Uncle Joe bursts through the crowd and picks up Devil Dog and we're all laughing and crying and barking. From the corner of my eye I think I see Guy, but when I look, he's gone.

Then Dick comes out of nowhere, breaks up our frivolity and says, "It's about time, Swanson. We have work to do. You have everything?"

Devil Dog? Check. Suitcase? Check. Clarisse Barnum's divorce file? Oh, oh.

"I've got to go back to the plane," I say, excitedly. "I left some important papers there."

"You can't go back in," Dick says.

"It's important, Dick."

"Well, what is it," he asks, exasperated.

"Clarisse's divorce file."

He groans. "Everything?"

I nod. "The attendants will probably just throw it away. It's only paper, right?"

Dick looks at the swinging double doors, undoubtedly trying to figure out a way to get in, but it's hopeless. Even I know that. "You need a system, Swanson, so when you have to move quickly, you don't leave things behind."

I never heard him sound nervous. "I'm sorry, Dick."

"Sometimes you just have to rely on luck. Let's hope we're on a winning streak, Swanson."

"I owe you," I say.

"You bet you do. And you can start now."

Chapter 13

The Bark Is Worse Than The Bite

Dick pulls me away from my uncles who shout, "Bring her back for dinner! We have a special dinner planned. Bring Clarisse, too!"

I wave to them as Dick tugs me down an escalator and out the door to a taxi stand, where he's brazenly parked a Peugeot station wagon with blinkers on. He says something to a gendarme in French. He speaks French? Of course he does. The gendarme salutes him smartly and clicks his heels and touches the brim of a very snappy looking cap at me. Devil Dog and my luggage are stashed in the back, and away we go.

"Who do they think you are, Dick? Hercule Poirot??"

"Swanson," Dick says, "I am a professional private detective, here in France on a very visible case. I have worked here before. The French respect detectives and what we do."

We exit De Gaulle onto an elevated speedway above what I guess are the Paris suburbs, turn onto the beltway that surrounds Paris and soon we're cruising along the autoroute in the French countryside and as tired as I am I feel my heart beating faster as I look out the window. I'm in France! It's wicked gorgeous. Freedom fries be damned.

"Pretty beautiful, isn't it," Dick says. "When you're seeing a place for the first time you're all eyes. You don't have preconceptions about the people who live there yet. That'll change when we get there so enjoy the view."

"Where are we going, Dick?"

"To the Meriodoc's chateau in Orléans."

"The Meriodocs have a chateau?"

"Michel Meriodoc is—was—descended from a family that dates back to 1500."

Devil dog climbs over the seat and perches on my lap. Dick lowers the passenger side window so Devil Dog can rest his chin on the edge and yap as we race down the autoroute—French for turnpike?—at what seems like a hundred miles an hour. As fast as we're going, cars are passing us.

"Don't they have speed limits in France?"

"Depends on the road. They're not as controlling about some things as we are."

The scenery, well, I'll try to describe it. Ours is like Davy Crocket—wild, untamed, awesome, the Grand Canyon, right? Theirs is tamed to a kind of perfection. Like they've been cultivating it for a few thousand years and have worked out the kinks. Which is awesome, too.

Dick is carrying on a non-stop history lesson—Marcus Aurelius, Joan of Arc, both of whom claimed Orleans as a home— and I nod to let him know I'm listening because I can't look away from the scenery. Farmland and vineyards and then a village built up a hill so steep that it looks like the houses are piled on top of each other with a walled fort at the top or a church with giant spires pricking at the sky.

In no time at all we're crossing into Orleans over a bridge that Dick says the Romans built. We drive along a river—the Loire, Dick tells me—past beautiful old buildings that you know are hundreds and hundreds of years old and I think to myself that I can never call Beacon Hill historic again.

Then we cross out of the city over another bridge and back into the scenery. We leave the main road for a country road which turns into a dirt road. I'm holding Devil Dog tight to keep him from bouncing out of the window. Suddenly, we turn onto an unmarked single lane you could drive right by if you didn't know it was there. We pull up to a gate. Dick gets out and presses a code into an alarm box and the gate swings slowly open. We'd gotten here at mach speed but now Dick downshifts to second gear and we're driving at like five miles an hour. Ranks of closely planted plane trees stand at attention on either side of us forming a green canopy flecked with halos of sunlight over our heads. A man on a huge dappled work horse appears between two trees and reins back for us to pass. Devil Dog barks at his horse who paws the air with his hooves and sniggers a toothy neigh at him. His rider laughs. It's like we've entered some kind of magical kingdom. We crest a hill, come out of the woods and descend to a wide circular driveway and stop in front of a huge dignified ancient pink and white stone building. I stop counting after 30 windows. The front yard, I mean the front meadow, is manicured to the edge of the woods we just left.

"It looks like one of the mansions in Newport," I say. I went to Newport on a Boston Latin field trip.

"Very perceptive, Swanson. The Vanderbilts sent their architects here so they could reproduce these homes."

"Well, the Meriodocs can't be that wealthy. There's no moat."

I've been sitting forever. My back is killing me. I don't even know what I did with my shoes. I rummage under the front seat and finally come up with a pair of red patent leather Jimmy Choos. I can't remember wearing them on the plane. I tug them on and yawn loudly and stretch. The pills Guy gave me haven't worn off completely.

Two entitled looking French standard poodles, one champagne colored and one chocolate colored, come cantering out through a rose trellis. Both of them sport tiny red satin bows in the middle of their long ears.

"Chocolat and Edith Piaf," Dick says.

They and Devil Dog bark exhaustively at one another, have a huge butt-sniffing session, seem to like each other's brand of perfume, and they run off together, Devil Dog trailing his leash.

"I guess they won't go far," I say.

"I wouldn't count on it," Dick says.

A couple of seconds after the dogs disappear behind the house a chorus of yelping fills the air.

"Oh my god, what is that?"

"Basset hounds. The poodles and Devil Dog must have stopped by their kennel to say hello but the Bassets only understand one thing, tracking game. They're the estates hunting dogs.

"Hunting dogs? What do they hunt for? "

"Dinner. Rabbit, roe deer, wild boar."

"No turnips and beans for you?"

"I've been holding out but it's very hard to be a vegan in France. And hunting is actually a lot of fun once you get in the swing of things."

The swing of what things? Shooting dinner? Dick pulls my suitcase and Devil Dog's carrier out of the Peugeot and I follow him up the marble steps, pausing for a moment before we go inside. "It is really beautiful, Dick. The air. Even the smell is different, don't you think?" I am finding it hard to believe a man was killed here.

I close my eyes to enjoy the late summer sun when a high pitched screech sounds above our heads. A chill goes down my back. "What is that?"

"Michel Meriodoc's eagle owl Hannibal." Dick holds the door open for me. "We'd better get inside. He's been crazy with grief since the murder. And he's ferocious. If he could talk, he would lead us to the murderer. I have no doubt he knows who did it. Wait till you see him."

A giant shadow crosses the ground around us, but when I look up I'm blinded by the sun. I shade my eyes, but still can't see anything.

"Isn't an owl the symbol of the Athena Corporation?" I ask.

"Yes, but it's way too heavy handed a clue if that's what you're thinking. With the mood Hannibal's in I'll send one of the servants to find Devil Dog. Hannibal has been known to bring home a fox. A fully grown one. Although Devil Dog is probably safe with the poodles. Under their fancy curls they're hunting dogs too. And so are we."

Chapter 14

Black Definitely Does Not Agree With You

It takes some muscle for Dick to push the two big front doors open—once he gains momentum it looks more like they're pulling him—to reveal a white marble floored foyer with a towering ceiling and twelve foot high double doors to other spaces on both sides. The walls are painted a brilliant yellow orange and are covered with paintings. Along one wall is a wide marble and wrought iron stairway that ascends into the upper reaches of the house. Dick puts down my suitcase and Devil Dog's carrier.

"Tulane or one of the footmen will bring your bag to your room and they'll stash Devil Dog's carrier in the stable. He won't need it here."

"Footmen?"

"It's an antique house and they still use antique terms."

Maybe the wooziness I feel is from the sleeping pills or maybe it's because I feel like I should rehearse the lines for my part in a period movie.

"How many servants are there?"

"Clarisse told me they used to have twenty in service and cut back to nine including the chauffeur, the cook, and the game keeper. That was him on the horse we passed on the way in. Meriodoc's in there." Dick points to a side room. "It's his library. In his will he requested that his viewing take place in the room where he was most at home. He was a student of falconry and a dog genealogist. Falconry is…"

"Surprise… the owl and the poodles, I get it."

"There's a family cemetery on the estate. They were going to bury him earlier this morning, but Clarisse wanted to wait for me to get back from picking you up."

"Don't they have funeral parlors in France?"

"Swanson, this is a different world than you're used to. Maybe I should rent you a room in a hotel in Orleans till you get over the bends."

"Very funny."

"Wait for me. I want to tell Clarisse we're here. I'll be right down and I'll introduce you to the corpse." Dick bounds up the stairway taking two steps at a time.

I am left alone in the gigantic echo-y marble foyer—where is my faithful dog when I need him? My sense of awe is giving me goose bumps. Everything here is too big. I wonder if there's anywhere in this mausoleum where you can feel cozy. I nudge the door to the corpse's library open with my shoulder and peek in. Then I feel guilty so I try to pull it closed but it's too heavy. What the heck. My uncles taught me good manners, to respect to the dead, so I go in quietly as I can.

The coffin is on a small platform in front of a sofa. There's a tall wooden bookstand at one end of the coffin facing in with elaborate carvings of birds on its base. I assume the volume open on it is a Bible, but it's a genealogy about German poodles. Jeez! The guy doesn't seem to know he's been dead for four days. I step down off the platform, sit down on the sofa and look around. All four walls are covered with leather bound books in wood paneled bookcases that reach to a vaulted ceiling 30 feet high with rolling ladders on tracks in front of each of them. It's like the Boston Athenaeum. I take a deep breath to collect myself, step back up on the platform and look in.

The corpse is dressed in a cardigan sweater, green corduroys and riding boots, which seems like a casual way to enter the hereafter. I guess the French regard death with their usual je ne sais quoi. I see no evidence on his face, neck, or hands of a brutal murder, but undertakers are very good at covering up messy deaths.

He was a very good looking man. It looks like he died with a smirk on his face, like in the middle of a wry joke. "Hey everyone!" he seems to be saying, "It's moi! What does a guy have to do to get a drink around here?" A full head of chestnut curls. Pretty tall and quite slender, which I find funny for a man devoted to food. His hands are clasped over his stomach, like I've seen a million times in viewings in Southie, but instead of the expected rosary beads, he's clutching a rolled up parchment scroll that I can see has fleur de lis on it. Probably the family coat of arms or maybe a to-do list for the afterlife.

A tidal wave of fatigue suddenly hits me and I bend to the kneeler by the casket and rest my head on the edge. Just for a second, I tell myself, when I hear the door open.

"There you are!" Dick says. "What are you doing? I didn't know you had a ghoulish streak."

"I'm so sleepy," I say in a stage whisper.

Clarisse comes through the door right behind him and heads right over for me. "Swanson. I'm so grateful to you for coming," she says. She is wearing a long black chiffon shirt over a pair of skinny black pants. Her blond curls are pulled back in a careless ponytail. She looks pale and wan and gorgeous. Dick looks at her adoringly.

"Do you want to clean up before people arrive?" she asks.

"What people?"

"For the service."

"Ah, yes, of course." I can't believe they waited for me to bury the guy. I didn't even know him. "Where can I do that? Freshen up?"

A young girl, about 18 years old, appears out of nowhere with Devil Dog trailing obediently behind her, thank goodness, accompanied by Edith Piaf and Chocolat.

The girl is wearing a French maid's uniform exactly like you see on billboards for Gentlemen's clubs. "Follow me, Miss Swanson," she says, handing me Devil Dog's leash and leading me briskly out of the room.

Dick follows and grabs me by the elbow. "Be ready in half an hour. And don't act like a yahoo when you see your suite."

The maid picks up my suitcase from the foyer and heads up the stairs, the two poodles bounding ahead of her.

I pick up Devil Dog—stairs are not his strong suit—and we examine the paintings that line the brilliant yellow-orange stairway as we follow her. The portraits all bear a family resemblance to the dead dude in the casket. I groan. It would have been clean cut enough if Clarisse were just divorcing Meriodoc. Now that he was murdered there was no telling what family snakes would come slithering out from under the Meriodoc coat of arms.

The maid, whose name is Tulane, opens one of the doors in the long mirrored hallway and ushers me into my suite. She puts my suitcase in a grand hotel size bedroom and returns to the sitting room to open doors that lead out onto a balcony.

I gasp. The room is painted in various shades of new-leaf green and the crown molding and other wooden doodads are silver gilt. The furniture is an elegant dark exotic wood. Ebony, maybe? Whatever it is, it's as if someone peered into my soul, divined my taste and designed a room around it.

"It was just re-decorated," Tulane says. "We're restoring all the rooms, one at a time."

"We're?" I ask absently, noting that her English is excellent. Almost no accent.

Tulane blushes just a little. "Yes, we. My family has lived here for generations. My father still works here as well."

"Oh." So old French houses passed their servants down with the property. Like Gone with the Wind.

"Your mother?" I ask.

She bows her head. "She died when I was very young."

I feel sympathetic. "My parents died when I was five years old," I say. I almost never tell anyone.

Tulane shakes her head haughtily and says, "My father, as I said, is still alive. He is in charge of the autos. If you need anything, here," she says touching a thick woven cord behind a lounge chair. "It will call us downstairs. I will take your adorable dachshund and feed him. Such a shame the master didn't get to meet him." She picks up Devil Dog, who I am annoyed with because he doesn't seem to mind. The two poodles who exhibited good manners by sitting quietly at the door to the suite, stand up, and with that she's gone.

I go out onto the balcony. Beneath me is a pink stone terrace that runs the length of the building. I must be at the back of the chateau because there is no driveway, no cars. My suite looks out over a lawn of topiary creatures that starts at the bottom of a long wide set of steps that gives way to a gigantic maze that runs to a horizon of dense woods. I can see some out-buildings hidden in the woods and stands of trees and assume they're stables and garages and dog pens. Everything is so beautiful that I am surprised I feel like I'm in a prison.

A huge bathroom is off the bedroom and I start the water for a tub. What the heck, right? The tub's spigot is a dog's head. Naturally. Colorful bottles line a glass shelf attached to the side of the tub and I pick one up, smell it—rosemary?—and pour the contents into the bath and play with the bubbles as they form large sculptures. I let my clothes fall off my body and step into the tub and close my eyes, trying to fight off the jet lag and Guy's pills because I have a funeral service to attend.

I wake up to loud laughter and something that sounds like a party going on downstairs. I am in a canopied bed wearing a pink satin robe, not mine. I don't remember getting out of the tub. I jump out of bed, tie the robe closer around me, go out into the hall and peer over the railing where people are coming in through the front doors in seemingly jovial moods. I rub my eyes. Wasn't this supposed to be a funeral?

Dick is greeting people, but he feels my eyes on him, breaks away and comes up the stairs to me. "Swanson! We let you sleep."

"So I gathered."

"Do you feel like joining us?"

"Isn't this a memorial service?" I whisper loudly.

"Of course it is. Get dressed and come down. We're opening the champagne."

Chapter 15

For He's A Jolly Good Fellow

I don't know what funerals are like where you come from, but in South Boston, Massachusetts, we show some respect for the dearly departed. We don't go around popping champagne and talking World Cup. Well, until some renegade uncle brings out his pocket flask of whiskey. Then people start to sing. Then cry. Then talk about the Red Sox and the Patriots and the Bruins. Actually, now that I think about it, it's no different than what's happening here in a modest chateau in the middle of nowhere, France.

The library where Meriodoc had been laid out is filled with people. So many of them. Doors to another large room are wide open and that room is crowded too. Meriodoc himself, or what was left of Meriodoc, is gone, buried while I cavorted in bubbles then passed out. Someone cups my elbow. "What do you think, Swanson?" Dick whispers.

"I hope that my friends are a little sadder if I get popped," I say.

"Everybody's sad, but they've been drinking." Indeed, Dick holds a bottle of Dom Pérignon in his right hand. "Of course they're raucous."

"Then what?"

"Who do you think did it?"

I look around the room. "You think the person who killed Meriodoc is here?"

"Of course he's here. Or she. Murderers always want to see the effects of their handiwork."

"Well, I don't know anybody. I haven't spoken to anybody, and I haven't had a drink yet, because somebody is bogarting the bottle."

A male version of a French maid appears magically. Dick snatches a fluted glass off his proffered silver tray and pours me some bubbly. "Better?" he asks as I down it in one gulp. "Be careful, you're still jet lagged. You'll get drunk really fast. Clarisse is a mess and I have to take care of her. I'm counting on you to do some of the leg work for me."

"Like what?"

"Like, I think you should circulate and get to know people. Get in the swing of things. Get the lay of the land."

"I don't speak French. What if they don't like me?" I ask. Honesty lurks at the bottom of a glass of champagne. Let's face it, Americans don't like the French because we are certain they couldn't possibly like us. Probably an inferiority complex posing as overconfidence on our part. They're shorter but they're leaner and their hair is never mussed or cleverly so and their socks match their belts or neckties and they're never unshaven, at least their faces. I could go on but won't.

"They're going to love you," Dick says, pushing me towards a crush of people at a table overflowing with smoked salmon and confetti.

"Bonjour," I say in my champagne-enhanced French.

A middle-aged man and three young women in short skirts and scarves draped over their tank tops are engaged in an intense discussion and they act annoyed when I interrupt them.

"Swanson Herbinko," I say, sticking out my hand. "How do you do?"

One of the young women titters. "Chanel," she says while the other two women look up at the ceiling.

"Chanel? That's such a French name!" I squeal and the man looks at me in horror. "Well it is," I say. Jeez, what's in the champagne? I try to focus. "I am a friend of Clarisse's."

"Obviously," the man says then hisses to the others as if maybe I had wax in my ears, "Américaine."

If the killer is in this room, like Dick says, I hope it's this obnoxious guy. I wouldn't mind escorting him to the gallows.

Just then, a big guy, wearing a cowboy hat and boots walks into the room and stands in the doorway. Respectfully, he takes off his hat and looks around until he spots what he's looking for: Clarisse.

"Daddy!" she says, running over to him.

"Honey! I'm sorry I couldn't get here sooner," he says as he envelops her in his arms.

Daddy? That can't be her father. He's as ugly as Clarisse is beautiful. He's at least 6 foot 5 with thin straight blue black hair—obviously dyed—that lies at a flat smooth angle to cover his enormous forehead. I recognize it immediately as a comb over. His eyes are small and wide set and his rugged face is disfigured by acne scars. Combined with his western gear it makes him look slightly dangerous. Is this the guy with the motorcycle called "Daddy's Dream?" who made his family live in the foundation of a house while he spent all their money on Harleys? The man whose home Clarisse fled, falling into the hands of the Hell's Angels for a year? They haven't stopped hugging. Obviously, she's forgiven him.

"Has it been terrible?" he asks her.

"No, Dick was here with me and...Swanson." She smiles sweetly and gestures for me to join them.

Her father takes a couple of steps towards me and sticks out his hand. "Bill Barnum. Great to meet you, Swanson. My little girl has told me all about you. Thank you for taking care her."

I'm a little taken aback. Taking care of Clarisse didn't, historically speaking, seem to be number one in his priorities.

I'm just getting to know Clarisse," I say.

She's the best daughter a man could ask for."

"Daddy, I want you to meet Dick."

"Ah yes, Dick."

I step aside while this hulking mountain of a man shakes hands with his would-be future son-in-law who looks as stunned as I am that the fair and fragile Clarisse could be the spawn of this scarred behemoth.

The snotty French foursome that had dismissed me wander over and it's obvious by their flattering deference to Barnum that they're business underlings.

Suddenly I'm acceptable by association. The snotty male

introduces himself.

"How do you know Monsieur Meriodoc?" I ask Paul-Jean.

"I work for Athena Corporation."

"You mean the Athena Corporation? The one that is trying to get France to allow importation of Frankenfood?"

"That's such a typical American remark," Paul-Jean says. "Americans are expert at reducing complicated arguments to slogans. It's some kind of genius, maybe?"

The women laugh.

"Frankenfood, as you call it, is responsible for feeding large portions of the world's hungry," Bill Barnum says. He hitches up his pants like a cowboy and is suddenly talking in a drawl. "It's all about high-yield. The world's population is exploding, there is no other way to feed everybody. It's called progress. I can't help it if certain parties don't get it."

"Certain parties like Michel Meriodoc, you mean?" I ask.

Bill Barnum laughs and pokes his finger at me. "She's an attorney, how do you people say it, an avocate? She probably thinks I killed Michel because he wouldn't give his consent to allow importation of Athena's product." Suddenly I'm not his darling daughter's savior.

Paul-Jean sniggers. "It's so American to think that. If you don't approve of something you pull out your gun and settle the score. Bang, bang! The French are more civilized than that."

"Obviously they are," I say. "Much more civilized. Oh, now wait? Didn't the French murderer use a gun?"

"You don't know it was a Frenchman," Paul-Jean says.

"You don't know it wasn't," I say.

Paul-Jean turns away from me—God, I hate that guy!—taking Bill by the arm and leading him into the adjacent room. The women stroll after them like virgin acolytes. Clarisse catches up to them and puts her arm through her father's, Dick in her wake.

Bill Barnum. His booming voice carries even from the other room. I am thinking about what Dick told me: the murderer was probably in this room. It seems odd that old Bill hadn't bothered to meet his daughter's boyfriend until today. Maybe he was too busy planning to kill his ex-son-in-law. Stop being ridiculous, I chide myself. You're just tired. It was more likely that little French creep, Paul-Jean.

And what about Clarisse? At my office she'd given me an anti-Frankenfood lecture. Not a word out of her mouth. Hmm. I was getting the lay of the land and it made no sense to me.

Someone touches my arm gently and I turn around to see a young man about 35 years old who bears a startling resemblance to Michel Meriodoc.

"I am Sébastien Meriodoc. Michel's son," he says, needlessly, because talk about the apple falling not far from the tree. "This is my wife, Sylvie."

A woman with her black hair clipped up in a twist and wearing all black and a scowl clings to his side. A smudge of fuchsia lipstick tries to create the full set of lips that nature didn't bestow on her. She offers me a hand that feels so small I think I might crush it if I grip it, so I pat it instead and end up patting a humongous diamond ring. She reluctantly raises her head and I can see the shiner on her right eye under tons of make-up.

"I am so sorry for your loss," I say.

"Don't be," Sylvie says. "Maybe now that the old fool is dead Sébastien can finally do what he wants with his life."

Sébastien shrugs. "I love what I do. It's fine."

"And what is that?" I couldn't remember anything Dick or Clarisse said about Sébastien other than he wouldn't mind a windfall from his father's estate, but who wouldn't?

"My husband is a farmer. You have to be crazy to want to farm, especially the way his father encourages him to, like it's the dark ages. You get up at three thirty every morning. Even in winter there's some goddamn horse that is foaling. In bed at eight. When was the last time we even went to the cinema?" Sébastien gives her a look as if he's measuring to give her a matching shiner on her left eye. But she's undaunted. "It's not what I signed up for when I married him, I can tell you that."

"What did you sign up for?" I can't help asking.

"Look around." Sylvie makes a sweeping gesture with her free hand. "This place is nice. It's nothing like I live in. Let's put it that way."

"You're a farmer's wife," Sébastien says. "I was up front with you, wasn't I? Farmer's don't live in chateaus, even though our farm is on the estate. You can't raise hens in a maze."

"The chateau is finally yours now, though, isn't it?" Sylvie says

58

triumphantly.

Sébastien lowers his head. "If everyone wants to stay, I can stay here. If not, we have to sell. The farm is separate though."

"Everyone? What do you mean, by everyone?" I ask.

"There's Clarisse to consider. And others too."

I want to ask who these others are but Sylvie isn't finished.

"You see, though, Swanson—that's your name, right—my husband isn't really a farmer bringing in cash crops. He just does experiments for his father. For his father's fixation with terroir. Saving seeds so generations from now the people who live in the Loire Valley can eat the same things their ancestors ate 500 years ago. Always looking back."

"That's not all we do," Sébastien says.

"That's all he'll let you do, you mean," Sylvie says. "The other stuff you have to do in secret. Everything's a big secret because the great white father, Michel Meriodoc, doesn't approve. He would rather have his grown son dependent on him forever than risk his reputation for being pure."

"That's enough, Sylvie," Sébastien says.

A waiter arrives with a tray of champagne flutes and Sylvie takes one and puts a finger on his sleeve to make him stay, swigs it down immediately, puts the empty on the tray and picks up another, motioning with her head that he is dismissed. "That was the longest funeral I have ever attended."

Sébastien turns to me suddenly, taking my hands in his and whispering. "I would like to speak to you privately, Mademoiselle Swanson."

I nod and hand him my business card. Clarisse no longer needs my services but here is a man who could use them. "I haven't tried my phone here, yet, but send me an email. I don't practice law in France, you understand that, right?"

"I don't know why we can't live in a nicer place when the rest of your family lives like royalty." Sylvie tries to grab another flute of champagne from a passing tray but Sébastien pulls her away with him.

I give him a thumbs up but he doesn't look back.

Michel Meriodoc certainly had his enemies, I think. And people's bitterest enemies are usually within swinging distance on the family tree.

Most of the guests are filing out. The platter of salmon *fumé* is empty and the butler who passed out the champagne is smoking a cigarette at the top of a stairwell that must lead to the kitchen with his hip resting on the door jamb. Suddenly he straightens up as if his boss caught him smoking and extinguishes his cigarette in the ash tray he holds in his other hand before disappearing down the steps.

Tulane, sweeps past him with another maid, gives her cleanup orders then walks out into the foyer and stands talking to Sébastien with her hand on his arm. Sébastien pats her shoulder and says goodnight and drags Sylvie who is in the middle of what is obviously an angry sentence up the stairway so I assume they are staying the night somewhere down the giant hallway from me. I picture Sylvie barricading herself in her suite. If she has to, she'll take the chateau by eminent domain, a subject I know something about.

Clarisse and Dick wander out of the adjoining room arm in arm, and engrossed in each other they too start up the stairway. Chanel and the other women I met talk earnestly on a corner divan, twirling their scarves in unison around their fingers. Bill Barnum and Paul-Jean are nowhere to be seen.

I feel like the only person on the planet who isn't paired off when a slight man with chin-length blond hair and a soul-patch under his bottom lip saunters into the room and I feel the air acquire a lighter weight than it had so far and I laugh. Guy de Guy!

He smiles at me and raises an index finger in greeting before I run up to him and let him kiss me: left cheek, right cheek, left cheek again.

"Three times?" I ask him. "You French are so thorough! Not complaining, mind you…"

"Shut up," he says and kisses me right on the lips.

Chapter 16

Amazing Developments

"I am so glad to see you!" I whisper in Guy's ear.

He laughs.

"Is your sister okay?" I ask.

"I don't understand her."

"She's not leaving him?" That is so typical of women. He may be a bastard, but he's my bastard. He didn't mean to hurt me, he was drunk, he was high, he usually kicks the dog but the dog was hiding under the bed. There are a million reasons to hit a woman, it seems, none of them good. And none of them have anything to do with the woman, yet women always think they deserve it somehow.

"I'm sorry," I say. "I don't know how to help. Unless she needs a friend? I know social services in America. I don't know what you have here. "

"She wouldn't go anyway," he says. "She's under his spell. And I am embarrassed to say that part of the magic is a fortune."

He looks around at the remains of the party. There are a few people still drinking in the far room and Bill Barnum's girl lackeys are still in the corner talking. Everyone else who is staying at the chateau has wandered off to bed or other parts of the house or grounds.

"Were there lots of important people here?" he asks.

"Some people who thought they were important." It seems a funny question to ask. "Did you know Meriodoc?"

"Quite well. Professionally, of course. For my blog, you know.

Nothing says lifestyle to a Frenchman like food. Food and politics are the twin passions of French life."

I never even think about politics, much less talk about it. Food, however....I could get something going there. I fell for Guy over a roasted duck, for pete's sake.

"Are you staying here?"

"I was invited to the service, so yes. I've stayed here many times."

I see Dick through the doors that open onto the terrace talking earnestly with Bill Barnum. How many stairways does this place have? Clarisse is standing between them. She says something that makes them both laugh then puts her arms through theirs and they walk out of sight.

"Do you want to take a walk around the grounds?" I ask Guy.

"A good idea. It's a beautiful evening."

Tulane, who is loitering by us, says, "Excuse me, Monsieur Guy, just so you know since you're going for a walk, the garage where Monsieur Michel was killed is off limits."

While Dick is engaged in euphoria I am supposed to be getting the lay of the land. Why not check out the garage with Guy? "I'm sure the police have been over it a zillion times," I say to Tulane.

"My father is in charge of the vehicles and he's been told by the police not to allow anyone in. It's not a tourist attraction," she says, looking at me.

"*Bien sûr Bien sûr.* We understand, don't we Swanson?"

See, here's the thing with servants. When you're raised blue collar, like me, you're basically a servant yourself so it's very uncomfortable for me to assert authority over another working woman, who is bound to say, "and who do you think you are?" and then it would escalate into a cat fight. In situations like this I find that passive aggression works best.

I smile sweetly at Tulane. "Yes, of course we understand. Thank you so much for telling us. We won't go near it! Oh look, Tulane. There's a dirty fork on the floor right under that chair." I brush by her out onto the terrace. Guy follows and we stroll hand in hand down the steps and out into the topiary garden.

"My, my," Guy says. "The swan has claws. She's only a maid."

He leans against a tree, takes out a crumpled pack of cigarettes, taps one out of the pack and offers it to me.

"I don't smoke," I say. "Actually, no one I know smokes."

He pats the loose tobacco back into its wrap and lights it up. "You are full of pronouncements."

"Just saying." I feel like a complete dork so I change the subject.

"I want to see the garage where Meriodoc was murdered. Do you know where it is?"

"Yes I do, thrill-seeker, let's satisfy your curiosity."

He squeezes my hand and guides me through the topiary onto a grassy path through woods. I get a funny feeling that Tulane has come down the terrace steps to follow us when running down the path after us is Devil Dog.

"Hey, boy!" I yell. "Where've you been?"

Devil Dog runs up to me, tail wagging. I pat and hug him and he extricates himself from my grip and walks ahead of us sniffing the ground. I wish I felt as in my element as he seems to be.

To our right is a long sculpted hedge, at least 8 feet tall.

"What's behind there," I ask.

"It's the maze. All these chateaus have mazes. If the king has one, everyone must."

"I've gotten lost in corn mazes around Halloween when I was in high school. We would go there to make out."

"Same thing here," Guy says. "Except they used to wear powdered wigs and bustles instead of skeleton costumes. Actually, it is exactly the same. A good blog post, I think." He pulls out his iPhone and punches something in. "Making a note. I a-maze myself. Get it?"

"Hey, look, the garage is right ahead of us." It had been invisible as we were walking through the woods. It's a long white and pink stone building that is a replica of the chateau.

"The murderer could have hidden in the maze until he heard Meriodoc's car pull up. Maybe he's still out there," Guy says teasingly.

I swallow. A giant moon is shining above us in a blue silver sky. Devil Dog barks at it. I picture the whole thing. The killer poised in the maze—ready to vanish if someone suspects he's there. Meriodoc coasting down his driveway in a fancy sedan, the engine so quiet no one in the chateau hears him arriving. The garage man, Tulane's father, welcoming him home then saying good night and going up a flight of stairs to his living quarters. The killer hears the engine shut off. Meriodoc is jotting something into his iPhone. The garage door is open. The killer slips in. Meriodoc looks up in surprise. He know his killer. Of course. It's an inside job. The killer bends into the car, they exchange a three cheek kiss, and then the killer gives Meriodoc a smile, makes sure he knows what is about to happen to him, and shoots him in the back. Jeez, what a rotten surprise. I see that smirk on the corpse's face, as if he died hearing the punch-line of an ironic joke.

"Swanson, snap out of it," Guy says.

I try to get my bearings. We're right on the edge of the woods. Devil Dog is growling at something above our heads. A swooshing noise like a witch in a long cape is flying through the trees and I look up to see a giant bird bearing down on us. I drop to my knees, snatch up Devil Dog, clutch him to my chest and cover my hair. The creature lets out a scream and banks up over the garage roof.

Guy touches my shoulder then helps me up.

"Was that Hannibal?" I ask.

"You know about Hannibal?"

"Dick told me."

"He was after Devil Dog. Meriodoc loved birds of prey. He couldn't love something he might eventually eat. Hannibal was his pet. I think he spent more time at night with that owl than with his wife. I wrote an entire blog post about Meriodoc training Hannibal like a medieval falconer. It went viral. You know, if we're going to be friends, you're going to have to read my blog."

I'm ready to pee myself. My dog was almost owl dinner, and Guy is talking shop like things like this happen to him every time he takes an evening stroll.

We survey the sky for Hannibal, but he's disappeared.

"Let's go," Guy whispers and pulls me towards the garage which I see is long enough to house ten cars. The garage doors are old fashioned, not electrified. They're on tracks and slide. Guy gets up on tiptoe to peer through a window.

I jump up to look too, but I'm too short. "Give me a boost, will you?"

"Why don't we just open this door?" Guy asks, turning the knob. The door hinges let out a squeal.

"Shhh," I say.

"Don't shush me. I can't help. The door squeaks."

The moonlight is slanting into the garage and glancing off a row of beautiful shining shapes lined up from one end of the garage to the other. "Wow," I say.

"Shhh," Guy says.

But it's too late. Devil Dog barks at a tall figure who appears at the bottom of a stairway behind a Citroen sedan. I jump.

We all examine each other, until finally he recognizes Guy.

"*Bonsoir, Monsieur Guy, Suis-je vous aider?*"

Chapter 17

The Car Whisperer

Guy and the old man say stuff in French while I look on helplessly. Devil Dog growls at the man and it's all I can do to keep him from biting his leg.

"I'm sorry," I say to no one at all, because no one is listening. "He usually isn't like this. Devil Dog, behave!"

Their conversation escalates to an argument and finally Guy says to me, "He doesn't think I should be here."

"Why"

"The blog, you know?"

"He doesn't like your blog?"

"He knows I like Meriodoc and he doesn't think I should be snooping around."

"What do you mean, you like Meriodoc? I thought you just wrote about him."

Guy cups my elbow. "Come on. We should leave. I don't want to get into a fight just to satisfy your curiosity."

"I'm not ready to leave," I say shaking off Guy's hand.

"Vous êtes américaine?" the old man asks me.

"Oui!" I answer, happy to be part of the conversation at last.

"I love America!" the old man says in accented English. "No bullcock in America."

"I think you mean bullshit, Theodore," Guy says.

"Is that right?" he asks me. "Bullsheet?"

"Yes, *oui*, that is correct, and you are?"

"Theodore Manescu. I am in charge of all the cars."

"Tulane is your daughter?"

"You are a friend of Tulane's?"

"We're not like best friends or anything. I just met her."

"Americans don't have class bullsheet like here. I listen to your Armed Forces Network. Everyone the same."

"Ah." So that's where he gets his information. From my personal experience, I know that if a group of lawyers are talking, there is no better conversation stopper than having one of the lawyers admit—humbly, but insistently—that she graduated Harvard Law. Implying that all the others aren't worth naming. If that isn't class bullsheet, I don't know what is, but I'm not about to undeceive him. "We try to live up to our ideals," I say.

"She wants to look in the car Monsieur Michel was murdered in," Guy says.

"There is nothing to see. The gendarmes have been all over it. Looking for what I don't know."

"Probably a bullet casing," I say.

Theodore shrugs. "Not my business."

"Which of these beautiful cars was he shot in?"

"His favorite. There." He points three cars from where we're talking. "The Bentley. He liked English cars best, and it's not my job to complain how much time I spend fixing them. English cars are bullsheet. And now I can't get it to start. It's as if when Monsieur Meriodoc died the car lost its will to drive. It never liked me because I didn't like it and now it just won't go."

"You're saying the car is sad that Meriodoc is dead?" I ask.

"I can tell what's wrong with a car by putting my ear to the hood and just listening. Nobody listens to cars. But the Bentley doesn't want to be started and who am I to insist? It's not my car."

So here we are in the garage where a celebrity food guy was murdered like three days ago, the murderer not yet caught and as far as I knew no suspects—or nothing but suspects—with this batty guy who fancies himself a car whisperer.

"Did you like Monsieur Meriodoc?" I ask.

"Bowf!" he says, using an expression I've heard since I've

arrived in France when people are exasperated. "He was my supérieur. France is not America. I worked for him. I will work for whoever owns the house, you know? The Manescus have been employed by the chateau for generations."

I laugh. "Everybody hates their boss."

"That's not why I hate him," he says, surprising me.

"So you do hate him?"

"Of course I hate him! But not because I work for him. Because he thinks he is better than me. Better than my family."

"Oh." Class warfare in France, where, if I'm not mistaken, they had a guillotine set up to stop it. "Do you have a gun, Theodore?"

"You can't trick me," he laughs. "The gendarmes tried that too. If I killed everyone who thought they were superior to me, there would be nobody left in France. But if I wanted to, there are rifles everywhere. I could just pick one up and bam!" He hoists an imaginary rifle to his shoulder, follows a ghostly duck, and knocks it out of the sky.

"Really? I thought France didn't allow people to own guns."

"This is a hunting estate. There are so many guns here we don't even count them anymore."

It was hard to believe that someone would just saunter into the garage carrying a loaded rifle. Although, as my eyes adjust to the dark, I can see a rifle on a rack on the wall below a stag head. There is space beneath it for another one, which just happens to be not there. Who would have known about those rifles on the wall besides Theodore and Meriodoc himself? Apparently everybody.

"So, now that Meriodoc is dead, who are you going to work for?" I ask.

"Ask him," Theodore says. "Monsieur Lifestyle."

"I don't understand," I say. "What does any of this have to do with you?"

"I named Meriodoc the most influential person in France last month."

"You think someone was so offended by that, they would kill him?" I ask.

"Maybe if they thought they were more important. My rankings are very prestigious in France."

I can see that Guy is getting impatient with my being not at all impressed with his place in the pantheon of lifestyle gods.

"Of course," I say. "Who wouldn't want that honor?"

Theodore laughs. "I like you. You're not snobby like most of our visitors."

I don't know if I consider that a compliment or not. Being in a chateau for the last nine hours has made me yearn to be a little snobby.

Theodore goes over to a work table, opens a cabinet and takes out an unlabeled green bottle. Taking out a pocket knife, he whittles around the cork and opens it, then rummages in the cabinet again taking out three Baccarat crystal goblets which sparkle in the reflected moonlight.

"Join me?" he asks.

I nod and he pours too much in each goblet.

"Nice glasses," I say. "I guess the pay is good here."

"I took them from the house. Why shouldn't I drink from nice glasses, eh? "

"No reason at all," I say, taking a sip of the wine. "Wow, it's nice," I say.

Theodore squints at me. "You know about wine?"

I take a big swallow. "No. Not at all. All I know is it makes me tipsy." I hiccough.

"It's from the Saint-Emilion estate. You know it?"

"I know it," Guy says. "It was a scandal I'll tell you about sometime, Swanson. But, if you want to know who Theodore is going to work for from now on, it's me."

"You?"

"Not me exclusively, of course. He's going to work for me one quarter of the time."

I look at Theodore who shakes his head in assent. "Somebody, please! What's going on?"

"It's French law," Theodore says. "It's beautifully precise and completely unfair. No?"

"I wouldn't say it's unfair," Guy says. "I made Meriodoc. He got lots of opportunities because I made him famous. The roof in this chateau doesn't leak because he got lots of money from those opportunities. Without me, he would be just another house poor aristocrat earning a pittance by taking in tourists. So, no, I wouldn't say the law is unfair at all."

"Clarisse and Sébastien don't get everything?" I ask.

"Under French law, she is only entitled to one quarter. Sébastien gets half. And the other quarter, Meriodoc could choose to dispose of any way he wanted without being challenged. And he chose to give it to me. For services rendered." Guy raises his goblet. "It's all marketing and branding, you know."

"Eh, bien." Theodore pulls out a rolling stool from under the cabinet and sits down and crosses his arms over his chest as if he's about to enjoy a good conversation, then remembers his manners and refills our glasses. "You are supposing, of course, that Sébastien is Meriodoc's only child. No?"

Guy says "Clarisse didn't have any children."

"Clarisse!" Theodore laughs. "She is not the only woman in France with a womb."

Guy's face goes white. "What are you trying to say, Theodore?"

"I'm not trying to say anything. I am just informing you that the monsieur has another child on the way." He takes a long drink, wipes his mouth on his sleeve, and smiles, enjoying making us wait. "My daughter Tulane is going to have Michel Meriodoc's baby."

Chapter 18

Three Is Always A Crowd

Guy and Devil Dog and I exit the garage in silence. Theodore sees us off from the doorway roaring with laughter and gulping straight from the bottle. Guy informs me as we walk toward the chateau that fifty years ago the owner of the Saint-Emilion vineyard fathered an illegitimate boy child and it took most of the grown man's life and all he'd ever earned as a pharmacist to claim his name and his inheritance.

"So is there going to be a fight over this?" I ask Guy. "I mean, you obviously feel gypped, but you still get something."

"Well, who is going to finance the Manescu's court costs? They would have nothing without me. I made Michel Meriodoc. I made him! Without me, he wouldn't have been elected president of the French Farmer's Association. He couldn't pay me while he was alive. That would have been inappropriate. I had to wait till he's dead, and then his screwing around, which I wasn't aware of, screws me. All for some little tart."

"Right. Well, first of all I want to remind you that I'm a woman and I don't like your attitude."

"Oh, please Swanson. I think worse of him that I do of her. Now there is a monkey wrench in what was strictly a business deal."

My elation over our fledgling relationship was badly deflated. Guy hadn't been up front with me and he had a huge motive to want Meriodoc dead. Sooner rather than later.

"How badly do you need Meriodoc's money?"

"My, aren't you the little detective. You think I had anything to do with Meriodoc's murder? I wouldn't kill anybody over money."

"We hardly know each other so why shouldn't I think it?"

Guy takes both my hands. "I swear to you I had absolutely nothing to do with it, Swanson. I need you to believe me."

I look into his blue eyes and down to the soul patch under his lip. I need to believe him, too. I want to believe him. "I believe you, Guy," I say, hoping that saying it aloud will make it true.

Dick always harps on hard evidence being the only evidence you can count on when you're dealing with criminals—or divorcing people, same difference—and the one thing I could believe is that there was no hard evidence in this case whatsoever. No smoking gun. No gun at all, for that matter. I shyly take Guy's hand. Innocent until proven guilty, right?

"Thank you, Swanson," he says.

I think we're going back to the chateau so I can catch up on my sleep, but Guy is distracted by a light shining in the woods. "Look over there."

"What's that?" I ask.

"The hunting lodge. Where they eat and drink after a hunt is over."

"It's part of the chateau?"

"A lot of people are staying over. Some of them are probably having a party."

"Who could be having a party after a funeral?"

"There's nothing like someone else's death, my little Swan, to make you feel like partying. Because you're still alive. Let's see who's there." He grips my hand and maneuvers me through the woods until we come to a wooden lodge that is as large as a triple decker in South Boston. The place is blazing with orange candlelight although it's awfully quiet for a party.

Guy drags me into the foyer. The ceiling is 15 feet high and the walls are covered with racks of antlers. On one wall is a tapestry of a hunt, like you see in museums, with stags and deer dying with arrows stuck in their shoulders or being torn apart by hunting dogs. Devil Dog is agitated by the scene. He growls and jumps around and I have a hard time keeping control of him without a leash. I can feel the intense blood lust and the chaos of death and I feel like gagging.

"I don't feel so good," I say.

"You eat meat, don't you?" Guy asks. "How do you think it gets from the ranch to the stockyard to the Styrofoam trays in the meat department of the supermarché? It's not like what's on these walls but it's just as bloody."

"I know you're right," I say. "Just give me a minute." My uncles are in the meat business, for pete's sake, so there is no rational argument for my repulsion at the details of where it comes from.

Guy pushes open a heavy wooden door and we step down into what looks like a conversation pit in a McMansion except this one has sofas and chairs with antler arms and gigantic tapestry cushions with hunt scenes on them.

Dick, Clarisse and Bill Barnum, are huddled around a table with tree branch legs talking, a cluster of open wine bottles in front of them. They seem startled to see us.

"Swanson, what are you doing here?" Dick asks.

"You asked me to come to France to help you find Michel Meriodoc's murderer. Remember?"

Dick looks from Clarisse to Barnum to Guy. His face is flushed. He's embarrassed. A first.

"All I asked you to do was to keep an eye on things for me when I wasn't in the chateau."

"Well, I was keeping an eye on things. In the garage. The crime scene. Remember? Guy chaperoned me. Hannibal tried to make a snack of Devil Dog as we were walking over and afterwards we had a nice little talk with the dead Monsieur Meriodoc's car honcho. He told us some very interesting information."

"That's enough, Swanson," Guy says.

"Please move over daddy," Clarisse says. She pats the depression where her father was sitting. "Come sit next to me, Swanson. Dick, pour Swanson a drink. She looks ill. What did Theodore tell you, Swanson? Theodore manages our fleet of autos" she explains to Dick and her father. "If he knows anything I want to know what. It's my husband who's been murdered."

"Well, he wasn't going to be your husband for long, dead or alive, was he. That's why you hired me. Remember?"

"That's enough, Swanson," Dick says.

Now if you asked me how this new tell-it-like-it-is Swanson

came into existence at this particular juncture: it's a no-brainer. I mean, if you're suddenly in a place where everything is like a movie set for *Les Misérables*, and you're pushed on stage with a bunch of people who don't even know you, but who nevertheless, every one of them, have a definite opinion about what you should and shouldn't do, know, think, feel, and your dog is attacked by a crazed owl in mourning, and you're jet lagged and pill silly, well, that's your answer. You gotta buck up. Circumstances make the woman. Someone said that, right?

"You shouldn't have been in the garage. No one is allowed in the garage. You probably polluted the crime scene," Dick says.

"Oh, Bowf!" I borrow their word. "Bullcock. The gendarmes would have left a guard at the scene if it was worth guarding. There wasn't a spot of blood anywhere, even in the car where Meriodoc was popped. The only one guarding the garage was the car whisperer who lives upstairs."

"Popped, Swanson? You watch too many detective movies," Dick says.

Clarisse lies back on the sofa and shuts her eyes.

Bill Barnum pulls a flask out of his black jeans and takes a long swallow. "Don't really like red wine," he announces. "Never did."

Devil Dog is pawing the sofa at my feet. I pick him up. He nudges into the space between me and Clarisse and finding it an uncomfortable squeeze jumps up on Clarisse's lap.

"Wine is about all they drink here in France," I say to Bill Barnum. "You might as well try to get used to it if you're planning to stay."

"Whiskey gives you clarity, young lady. The French should try whiskey," he says. "It would clear things up for them."

"What exactly do you think the French don't understand?" Guy asks.

"They don't understand the march of progress. They're against things they can't stop."

"You mean Frankenfood?" I ask. "Clarisse gave me a lecture in my office about how awful for you it is. You remember, Clarisse, right?"

"You mean your awful tiny office in Boston?"

"Hey, it's not that small!"

"You know what the first thing I do when I get out of bed in the morning is?" Barnum asks. "Every morning, before I brush my teeth and shower, I get down on my knees and I thank God I'm not French." Bill takes a long swig, wipes the mouth of the flask on his sleeve and offers it to Guy.

"I have news for you, Bill," Guy says, "Every day the French wake up and you know what prayer they say? They get down on their knees and they thank God they're not Bill Barnum."

Bill raises his flask to Guy. "Pleasure to meet you, too. Too bad your side is going to lose."

"I don't have a side," Guy says.

"Bull tail. No one's neutral. I've been reading your blog. I know you're against importing genetically modified grain."

"Really?" Guy says. "A great big strong man like you, going on the internet and reading? I'm impressed."

"Everyone, enough, enough! Shut up or I'm leaving," Clarisse says.

"Sorry, honey," Dick says, even though he hasn't been part of the symposium. "Everybody calm down and go to bed. We're sleeping in the lodge," Dick says to me, "Clarisse can't stand to be in the chateau. She's spooked because of the murder."

"Isn't that the murder with Athena's calling card next to the body?" I ask. I'm not ready to give up center stage. "That seems awfully suspicious, don't you think?"

"I'm being interviewed in Orleans tomorrow," Bill says. "If you're implying something, I'm not worried. Why would I kill Meriodoc? He's my son-in-law?"

"Was," I correct him.

Right! Was! Even more reason not to kill him. I guess, if I was going to be killing anyone, it should be old Dick here. Trying to steal my daughter before her husband's body is cold. A master suite in a chateau beats a two bedroom in Boston, eh Dick? I think he's the prime suspect, don't you?"

"Can't you just shut up, Daddy?" Clarisse asks.

"Sure princess. I don't mean to upset you." He sucks on his flask like it's a baby bottle and shakes a last few drops onto his tongue.

"So I guess you have free sailing now, selling the French GMO corn and soybeans," I say.

"Well, sugar, nothing's ever completely for certain, but it's looking a helluva lot better than it did a week ago. Meriodoc was the big obstacle in the path of progress. Let's just say, I'd be lying if I told you I was sad about the way things turned out. That youngin'? Sébastien? His wife is so hungry for a payday she'll make him do whatever I ask him to."

"No one seems really sorry Meriodoc's dead," I say to no one in particular.

"Swanson, that's so unfair," Clarisse says. "I'm completely distraught about it. Sure, Michel and I were divorcing, but I still loved him as a friend enormously. And I respected him. We were family."

"It's good you feel that way about family," I say, "Because your family is getting bigger."

"I know," Clarisse says. "Dick is going to make a great addition to our family."

"That's not the family she means," Guy says. "She means Tulane. Who is pregnant."

"What's that to me?" Clarisse says. "I never liked her. I would have let her go, and her arrogant father, except their family has been part of the estate for so long it would have caused a scandal and made Michel look like a monster. Tulane can have as many babies as she wants, girls like her always do. What do I care?"

"Well, she's part of your family now," I say. "Your dead husband is the father."

"That's impossible! Tulane? I don't believe it! " She looks around wildly. "Who would believe it?"

"Even serfs know about DNA testing," Guy says. "Damn those American cop shows."

"Does a bastard have a right to inherit?" Clarisse asks Guy, then Dick, then she looks at me, and all I can think is "why didn't I pay more attention to this kind of question in law school?"

Chapter 19

A Late Summer Night Rendez-vous

We leave the trio ruminating about Clarisse's diminished cut of the Meriodoc estate. It occurs to me that they can partition up the chateau with expandable baby fences like my uncles did to their apartment when they weren't speaking. I laugh out loud and Guy smiles at me.

"What?" he says.

In the lodge I'd crossed over from fatigue to performance like I used to do pulling all-nighters at Tufts before finals but all of a sudden the wine and chutzpah fuel are spent and I grab Guy's arm so as not to fall down. "Guy, I've got to go to bed. I am so exhausted I can't even pick my feet up."

"Poor baby," Guy says. "Let me give you a ride." He leads me gently to a two-foot high stone wall, boosts me up on it facing him and backs up tight between my legs. I put my arms around his shoulders and thrust myself onto his back but in doing so I accidentally kick Devil Dog who's right under us and he yelps and bounds away.

"Damn!" I say.

"Let's get him," Guy says. He starts running, staggering on the uneven ground, and I'm jostling and laughing so hard I feel like I'm going to topple off.

"Let me down," I yell, "I'm too heavy."

"Not at all, fair maiden," he says, following my errant dog along the edge of the woods. Devil Dog looks back at this unfamiliar horse and rider pursuing him and barks and Guy barks back, and Devil Dog deciding that discretion is the better part of valor turns and bolts into the maze.

I dismount and my steed and I gaze at the entrance to the maze. "Devil Dog," I holler. "It's me. Come back."

"He's gone," Guy says. "The maze is like two or three square city blocks and it's pretty complex. You don't have to worry, Swan. Dogs love it. The poodles sometimes disappear into it for days and they play cat and mouse games with people trying to find them. Dogs have some kind homing device that we don't. Devil Dog will find his way out by morning or we'll send out a search party."

"Well, I want to find him tonight," I say.

"You can't, Swan. You'll get lost. In Greek myth Ariadne had to give Theseus a ball of thread he could follow back out of the labyrinth after he killed the Minotaur. I don't want to scare you but people sometimes panic in mazes and get dehydrated and collapse."

"I don't care. Have you forgotten about Hannibal? I have to find Devil Dog before he does."

"Then wait here and I'll get a flashlight and go in with you."

"Alright," I say and Guy kisses my check and runs off toward the chateau. A big moon is shining overhead and the sky is textured with stars and the night air feels like a silky second skin. It's a magnificent fall evening but I haven't been my rational self since I left Boston and I am so so so tired, which explains why against all logic I am suddenly certain that Guy isn't coming back and without willing myself to move a muscle I forge into the maze.

The grassy corridor is just wide enough for two people arms entwined to walk along. The tall hedges on either side of me sparkle with moon dust but the pathway under my feet is dark. I immediately have to take 90 degree right and left turns and I come to a hedge wall dead end and have to turn back and take other rights and lefts and only maybe three or four minutes have passed and I'm already disoriented and lost.

"Devil Dog! Here boy!" I shout and I hear Guy shouting my name but his shouting seems far off so I don't bother to answer. I hear something rustling the hedges. "Devil Dog? Come here, boy!" No answer. I hear rustling again and think maybe it's rats. Of course it's rats. The corn mazes I used to go into to neck were full of rats. One of my boyfriends would bring an air pistol with him. "To protect you, not because I'm afraid. You understand that, don't you?"

I run my hand along the hedges to my left just to feel in contact with something and I almost fall into a break in the hedgerow. Great, I think and keep walking until I hit another hedge wall. I backtrack to the break and go through it.

"Devil Dog, come on. Please." I turn right, or is it left, and I hear rustling again and the hairs on the back of my neck stand up and I start to sweat. I'm not only lost. I'm scared too. I decide to walk looking up at the moon sprinkled tops of the hedges—the moon pops in and out of sight—and feel my way rather than trying to see where I am. This makes me feel in charge. My arms are out like a zombie's and I realize I'm about to lose it completely when I come out of a break in the hedgerow wall into a circular clearing with a fountain in the middle, water gently spilling over its sides into a little pond at its base. The moon is illuminating a bench against the hedgerow wall opposite and I walk around the fountain and sit down on the bench. The sound of the water splashing into the little pond is soothing and after a little while I get up and lean over the fountain and splash water on my face and drink from my cupped palms.

Calm down, I tell myself, just calm down. Guy knows you're out here. You heard him calling your name, didn't you? He's probably formed a search party and they'll be here any minute, but I should hear them shouting my name, shouldn't I, and I don't, and why would they bother looking for me? Everyone's mad at me for being a troublemaker and they've probably convinced Guy I'm not worth the time it will take to find me.

Don't be ridiculous, I chide myself. I'm in a maze that's only as big as a few city blocks that I could walk around in 15 minutes so what's to panic about? I close my eyes and take deep breaths and when I open them the night air which was smooth like a second skin feels a lot colder, probably because I'm sweating, and the little of myself I'd just managed to collect evaporates.

The temperature is plummeting, it'll be below freezing soon, these freak weather events happen all the time, and I'm going to die hallucinating because I hear voices carrying over the hedgerow I'm sitting against. I know I'm imagining them but I shout anyway: "Help! Help!" and I hear Devil Dog bark because he recognizes my voice and he's forgotten that I kicked him and dogs have built in radar, Guy said so. Devil Dog will lead me out of the maze. I don't need Ariadne's thread. I've got Devil Dog. I yell "Devil Dog, I'm here boy, for God's sake, find me," but he doesn't answer and there's stone silence and I realize my mind must have made up everything and I stand up to brush twigs and dirt off my clothing so when they find my corpse I won't look disheveled, and I hear voices again and I listen closely until I'm sure what direction they're coming from and the moonlight shining into the little oasis shows me there's an entrance back into the maze in the direction the voices are coming from and I walk through it onto a path without zigzags and I can make out that a man and a woman are arguing in French, and I'm suddenly scared that they are ghosts of dead lovers who got lost in the maze hundreds of years ago, but I shout "Help!" anyway and the arguing voices stop.

"Qui est-ce?" a male voice calls. "Is someone there?"

"Hello!" I shout. "I'm lost."

"I can't see you. I've got a lantern I'm going to turn up. Come toward it."

I see a flicker and I walk toward it until I come on two people outlined in moonlight sitting on a bench in front of me. Tulane and Sébastien.

"Why are you out here?" Tulane asks.

"I'm looking for my dog."

"She's lying. She works for Clarisse. You're spying on us, aren't you?"

"That's enough, Tulane," Sébastien says. "Mademoiselle Swanson is a nice person. We heard barking. Chocolat and Edith Piaf are out here somewhere. We thought it was one of them." He forms his two little fingers into a V, puts them between his teeth and gives a short piercing whistle and I hear rustling then I see Devil Dog running through the bushes toward me.

"There you are, boy!" I say bending down to pet him.

He's as happy to see me as I am to see him. His tail is wagging furiously. Tulane crouches down and pets him too. "You have a wonderful dog," she says. "I'm sorry for what I said. I haven't been feeling well since Michel died. I've got to get back before someone rings for me. Thank God, I won't have to put up with this much longer." Tulane stands up and stretches.

From what Guy had told me, Michel Meriodoc loved creatures more than he loved people. A farm girl like Tulane probably had more in common with him than an American sophisticate like Clarisse. In the moonlight she looks like a young harvest goddess or something and I realize I've been so self-absorbed that I hadn't noticed she's attractive. She doesn't look pregnant at all, but some women are like that. You can't tell until the last minute. Without saying goodbye she disappears into a hedge corridor in the opposite direction from the one I'd just come out of. Devil Dog starts after her. Sébastien gives a piercing whistle and he comes trotting back.

"Wow! Do all dogs come when you whistle?"

"Most do."

"I'm so glad I found you two," I say and sit down where Tulane had been sitting. "I was lost and panicking. I guess Tulane knows her way out."

"We grew up here, Mademoiselle Swanson. Even so, the maze sometimes fools us. It was created for a distant uncle of mine 500 years ago by the most famous puzzle maker in Paris."

I'm not panicked anymore and the brashness that had dominated me in the hunting lodge rears its head again. "So I'm guessing you two were out here discussing the monkey wrench her being pregnant by your father tosses into the inheritance game."

Sébastien looks surprised then he shakes his head and laughs. "I haven't heard American slang in a long time. I like it. Most Frenchmen like it but they pretend not to. How many people know about this besides you?"

"Let's see. Clarisse, Bill Barnum, Dick, Guy."

"If Tulane thinks she gets any of this inheritance, she's out of her mind."

"You're going to fight her?"

"Of course. Clarisse will. And Guy, too."

"Nothing will get distributed until they find the murderer," I say. "At least, that's how it's done in the States."

"It's no different here," Sébastien says.

"I'm sorry about your father, by the way," I say. "He seems to have gotten lost in all this."

"Not really. The rules are his. What any of us wanted is what has gotten lost."

"What will you do now?" I ask him.

"I will continue with my work. You know, I am not so young

that I can start over with a new career. Starting over is much harder in Europe than it is in America. And now, I have people waiting for the results of this year's experiments."

"What do you mean, experiments?"

"My work."

"I thought you were just a farmer. Sylvie said…"

"Sylvie's incredibly dramatic. I am a bio-engineer. And I am working on genetically engineered grapevines. And wheat, too. And corn and soy beans. I mastered rice, but we don't grow rice in France so it's hard to get support for that and I dropped it. I was hoping to go to market with my new seeds this winter in time for spring planting."

I stare at him until it becomes rude. "Excuse me? Genetically engineered?"

He laughs. "I hope you are not one of those people who get hysterical at the thought of genetically engineered food."

"No, I'm not actually. I don't know anything about it. I have other things to worry about. But I thought your father was opposed to importing genetically modified seeds from Athena Corporation."

"True, he was opposed to importing genetically modified seeds. I almost convinced him it was perfectly authentic to create our own. It's more authentic, no, to have foods that are produced au terroir."

"What's that?"

"Regional. Specific to the region. That's what I am doing."

"So your father just didn't want the competition?"

"No, father was a purist. In the end, I couldn't convince him. He threatened to give the farm to Tulane and pull the plug on my research. He thought it was immoral."

"GMOs?"

"Yes. GMOs are going to come here. There's no stopping them. So why should we always have American this and American that. We are perfectly capable of producing our own food. It's what we're known for. We're France!"

"So do you think it was somebody from Athena Corporation who killed your father?"

"Maybe. Probably. Who knows."

"You think Bill Barnum has anything to do with it?"

"I don't want to say. It could be anybody, you know? My father had a lot of enemies."

"I thought he was like the great white father of food."

"Guy made him into a star with his falconry and dog genealogy. Guy made father into something we in France thought we'd lost, an authentic French identity. In the end, we are just the story we tell about ourselves, no? Guy wrote papa's story and France fell in love with the hero Guy gave us."

"Hey, at the house this afternoon, you said you wanted to see me." His card was still in my bra.

"Yes, yes I did. You met Sylvie."

I nod.

"We met at college. In Boston."

"No kidding?"

"At Boston University."

"No kidding! I went to BU Law. We probably crossed paths."

"Probably nooooot," Sébastien says, and I'm suddenly aware of his expensive loafers and silk tan slacks. He was undoubtedly part of the Club X crowd: rich foreign students who partied hardy and expensively in private luxury condos on Boston Harbor. His family is aristocracy and he was raised in a chateau. I was named for a TV dinner which costs 99 cents and was raised in a triple decker in Southie. Where exactly would we have run into each other?

"Anyway," Sébastien says, "We got married in Boston and I want to divorce her. I thought you could do our divorce over there. So, will you take me on as a client? Dick says you're the best."

"Won't Sylvie contest this?"

"She will. But I have the money to wear her down. She has no resources so she'll settle sooner or later, don't you think?"

I'd been here before. "I guess, " I say. "Call me."

Sébastien gets off the bench and yawns. "I get up at three thirty every morning. It's amazing how light it is at three thirty, isn't it? Today, no sleep."

The sky's velvet black is turning silver. Maybe after a night's sleep I'll get some perspective on what I've been immersed in here. This whole trip to France has been one big surreal maze. And look at how I've been acting. I don't know whether to be pleased with myself or appalled.

"I'll come with you," I say. But just as I finish saying it a chorus of barking explodes to our left and Chocolat and Edith Piaf burst out of a maze corridor. They circle around Devil Dog then take off into the maze again and Devil Dog races after them. "Please no," I say.

Sébastien laughs. "They like your dog. We all do. Maybe you should leave him here and come back when you have my divorce finalized. Come with me. The poodles will bring Devil Dog along when they come out."

"I can't do that. Hannibal tried to eat Devil Dog earlier tonight. I have to find him."

"Alright, here," Sébastien says and hands me a hand drawn overhead map of the maze from his pocket. "We give this to every stranger who visits the chateau. I was going to give you a map when I saw you next, which is now. Listen to me. You know how trails are marked in the woods in Maine, don't you? Blue lines on tree trunks. The hedgerows are marked in blue, red, and white. You can't see the markings at night. We should have done them in Day-Glo paint but father thought that would be too American. Follow any one of the colors and you'll come out on one of the three sides of the maze that aren't up against the woods. I really don't think you have anything to worry about. Chocolat and Edith Piaf may look pretty but they're as ferocious as Hannibal when they need to be and Hannibal knows from experience not to mess with them. I have to go." A chorus of barking erupts nearby. "It's the three of them. Follow the barking."

I nod and he disappears between the silvery hedgerows and I think how nice it would be to fall asleep right here, under a hedgerow, when the three dogs emerge from a break in the hedges and race right past me. "Wait for me, boy," I shout and run after them.

I follow the barking like Sébastien told me to do. Sometimes it's close by. Sometimes it sounds far off. I'm alone again in a goddamn labyrinth that Theseus had to have a thread to follow to get out of and he was a super hero, and like it's been doing on and off all night my adrenalin cuts out and my exhaustion fills the void and it's still too dark for me to see the trial markings so basically I'm lost all over again. I decide I'll sit down right where I am. I'm not going to move till it's daylight and I can see. Why didn't I stay back on the bench where I was sitting with Sébastien? I sit down leaning against a hedge but before I can close my eyes Devil Dog is licking my hand and barking the little barks he gives when he wants to go out to do his business. He runs a little way down a maze corridor to my right, then stops and comes halfway back, barks and starts down the corridor again. I clamber to my feet and follow him. He repeats his come-with-me routine whenever I slow down and it's such a relief to be with him that I forget to be scared that I don't know where I am and play along.

This goes on for, well I don't know how much time, until we come to a bench like Sébastien and Tulane were sitting on. "Good boy," I say. "Good boy. Thank you for taking care of me." I think the game is over and I can sit down and wait for the dawn but it isn't. Devil Dog starts digging like mad at the ground underneath the bench with his front paws. He stops digging, barks at me and starts digging again. "What's going on. boy? Is there a bone buried under there that you want?" Chocolat and Edith Piaf probably have bones buried all over the maze.

He finally stops, sits down, looks up at me and then down at the hole, up at me then down at the hole, until I finally kneel next to him and see that what he's uncovered isn't a bone. It looks like the stock of a rifle. A stream of exclamations dance through my mind. Whoa, Holy Hanna, Caramba, Cheeze and Crackers, but I don't have time to make anything further of it because suddenly I hear the same noise overhead that I'd heard earlier—air whistling through a witch's cape—and silhouetted against the moon I see a giant owl flying overhead, its wing span casting a shadow over Devil Dog and me and the hedges around us. "Jeezums, no!" I cry.

I reach for Devil Dog to cover him with my body but he's whirling in a tight circle to keep the owl in his sight and barking furiously. Hannibal glides closer and closer, tightening the arc with each pass and suddenly he tucks his wings close to his body and becomes a bullet dropping towards us, screaming his horrifying cry. I hear a yelp. He has Devil Dog who is screaming and yowling with pain and confusion. Hannibal is having a hard time getting lift-off with him in his talons. He's dragging Devil Dog along the ground, and I am thankful I don't feed him Organic Dog. His extra girth from chocolate donuts is giving Hannibal fits. He lets go and readjusts his grip and I charge him, trying to yank my dog away. Devil Dog screams in pain and Hannibal sinks his beak into my hand. Rivulets of blood roll down Devil Dog's coat. "No!" I scream. I sit down on the ground. Tears roll down my cheeks. "My little dog. My little dog. Oh God, why did I come to this awful place?"

All of a sudden I feel two big creatures brush my legs as they whizz toward Hannibal and bang themselves against his body. Chocolat and Piaf! They bite at his wings and pull him off-balance until he's on his side on the ground shrieking and his talons miraculously open to release Devil Dog who runs whining to hide between them. Hannibal rights himself, hops away from us, disappears into a break in the maze shrieking indignation, and we watch him circle above us then fly away.

The two poodles lick Devil Dog's wounds and his face and bark encouragement at him and he tries to stand up but can't. Chocolat nuzzles Devil Dog and sits down tight against him as if to keep him warm. Edith Piaf races off barking loudly. I crawl over to the two of them and take off my jacket and cover Devil Dog with it and the three of us sit quietly as the sun ascends over the maze and I fall asleep. For how long I don't know. What I do know is that I wake up to voices and barking and open my eyes and Piaf and Guy and Tulane and one of the maids are beside us. Guy helps me up, looks at my hand which is bloody and swollen and kisses it.

"Swan," he says. "Why didn't you wait for me?"

I answer by bursting into tears and sinking my head into his chest. Tulane is kneeling by Devil Dog examining his wounds. She says something to the maid who came with her and the maid rushes off back into the maze. Tulane is saying comforting words to Devil Dog in French and he barks a little bark of appreciation. "Is he going to be okay?" I ask.

"I'll make some poultices for his wounds in the kitchen and I'll call the vétérinaire who takes care of the farm animals. You're going to be fine aren't you, little man," she says.

Chapter 20

Sunshine Always Used To Make Me Happy

Tulane's assistant bursts back into the opening with a big woven basket over her arm. She puts it on the ground in front of the bench and unpacks its contents: a boda bag full of steaming water, rags, gauze, tape, tubes of salve, a capped glass jar with some kind of yellow liquid in it, and a baster.

"Come here," she commands. "Sit facing me. You must hold your dog still. He isn't going to like what I am going to do and I don't want him biting me or squirming away. She scoops up Devil Dog, sits down on the bench facing out and puts him between us so quickly he doesn't have time to react. "Like this," she says clasping him across his shoulders and closing her hands tightly over his front legs. "Okay?"

I nod yes.

"Do it then." I grab him like she's just shown me but he starts to back out of my hands. "Hold him tighter," Tulane says. He's almost completely wiggled out of my grip. "Ah, he's not going to cooperate. Guy, venez. Vous le tenez."

Guy reaches down and clasps Devil Dog so tightly he starts to cry.

"Move Swanson," he says.

"You're hurting him,' I say.

"Allez! Allez! Move!" Tulane says. "We are not hurting your dog. Your dog is hurt. I'm going to give him a sédatif, clean his wounds, and we'll take him to the house and I'll call the vétérinaire."

"Donnes le moi!" she orders the maid who dips the baster into the yellow liquid in the jar, squeezes some in, and hands the baster to Tulane.

Guy adjusts his grip and presses both sides of Devil Dog's jaw just behind his teeth. "Open wide," he says and winks at me.

Devil Dog's clenched jaw opens, Tulane inserts the baster into his mouth, and squeezes its contents into his throat. Devil Dog tries to spit it out but Tulane clamps his jaw closed and finally he has to swallow. Maybe 15 seconds pass and all of a sudden Devil Dog stops fighting . "Bon," Tulane says and starts cleaning the four puncture wounds Hannibal left. When she's done she scoops Devil Dog up and deposits him in the basket, asks Guy to carry it, and the four of us plus the two poodles who have been sitting and watching, walk into the maze, and after innumerable lefts and rights we come out right where I'd rushed in.

It's uphill to the chateau balcony and Guy anticipating that I probably don't have strength left to make the climb puts his free arm around me and helps me uphill with my head on his shoulder.

"I am so happy you are safe," Guy says. He pulls me closer and kisses my forehead. "There is a killer here. And if the killer thinks you are getting close to discovering who he is, well, you are not safe either."

We reach the balcony. Tulane takes the basket from Guy and he leads me to a bench facing the morning sun.

"You're not going to believe this," I say, still resting on his shoulder. "Guess what Devil Dog dug up under that bench?" I try to repeat everything that happened but my body is so hungry for sleep I end up babbling. "Do you know how to get back to where we were so I can show you what we found?" I finally say. "Dick is probably up doing his morning sun salutations. Let's get him. Whosever fingerprints are on the gun is obviously the murderer."

Guy pushes me away and looks at me. His face which looked so affectionate a minute ago is ashen. "You are not going to mention this to anyone. Understand?"

"No, of course not. Well, you. I already told you." I get an uneasy feeling that maybe I shouldn't have told Guy before Dick. "Don't you want to find Meriodoc's murderer?" I ask.

"Of course. But things have to be straightened out first. "

"What things?"

"Things."

He stands and offers me his arm and I rise wobbling. "Let's get some food in you. We'll talk afterwards." We cross through the banquet hall where the funeral party was held and go down the stairs to the kitchen. Tulane is fixing giant pots of tea and coffee. Devil Dog is sitting on a chopping block eating out a dish filled with, I don't know what, French delicacies probably. I rush to him thinking how happy he'll be to see me. He looks up, gives his tail a single wag, and goes back to stuffing his face.

"I have called the vétérinaire," Tulane says. "He will be here in an hour to look at le petit chien. Your dog is going to be fine. You look horrible. Go to sleep and I'll wake you so he can look at your hand."

"A vet is going to look at my hand?"

"All doctors are the same," Guy says. "The ones who specialize in humans just charge more."

"Ah, oui," Tulane says. "Is this your cellphone? One of the maids found it in the salon. It was under a chair."

She hands me my phone which I must have dropped last night. The green message light is blinking. My uncles have called five times. Damn. They invited us to eat dinner with them when we got off the plane. I'd completely forgotten about them.

"Merci," I say, dialing voice mail. The first four messages are where the heck are you? The fifth is different. It's Uncle Joe. It's a rush of words all of which I don't catch so I replay it on speaker. "Swanson," he says. "If you get this before you've left to drive up here, don't come. There's a massive demonstration scheduled right by our apartment in the 20th this afternoon."

I pause the message. "What's the 20th?" I ask Guy.

"The 20th arrondissement. It's the neighborhood where your uncles live."

Uncle Joe continues. "The streets are full of students already. Some of them have slept here overnight. It's against American Frankenfood. Police wagons full of gendarmes have been arriving for the last couple of hours. Sacre blooey! We're going to watch from our window but stay away. You probably couldn't get within a mile of here anyhow. Some of our neighbors say they haven't seen anything like this since 1968. It's going to be a gigademo. Do you like that word? I'm going to send it to Merriam-Webster. We'll call you when the smoke clears. Au revoir."

Tulane pours me a cup of tea. "Miel?" she asks. "From our hives."

It's been a long night and I'm a long way from the Holy Bean on Beacon Hill.

Chapter 21

Take Me To Your Leader

"How did I not know about this?" Guy shouts. "That's what I get for chasing around after you. I'll bet Sébastien knows about this. Why didn't he tell me? What a moment this would have been for Michel. I'm going. I'll do a live podcast dedicated to his memory. I have to get my computer. You get some rest. I'll be back tomorrow. Au revoir."

The weird feeling I got from Guy's reaction about the gun has been displaced by an ache I feel because I'm not nestled on his shoulder. The prospect of sleep has become a distant hope. "I'm going with you," I say.

"You can't. You're exhausted. It may get violent. I'm going to be on the move the whole time."

I look at him forlornly. I make my lower lip tremble like I'm going to cry, a trick Uncle Stevie taught me. To use, he said, when your boyfriend doesn't want to spring for that pair of earrings.

"Alright. Alright. Be ready to go in 15 minutes. Tulane, do something for Swanson's hand," he says and rushes out of the kitchen.

Tulane washes my hand, pours something on the wound that stings like the dickens, "péroxyde d'hydrogène," she says. She brushes some goo on it from a jar on the windowsill, and bandages it. She hands me a fresh cup of tea and a croissant that I wolf down because Guy is already yelling for me from upstairs. I want to apologize to Devil Dog for leaving him behind but he's sound asleep.

I stagger up the stairs, Guy grabs my hand and we rush out to the driveway where one of the male servants has his Citroen already running. "Can you drive stick?" he asks.

I nod yes. Driving stick shift is one of my vanities. Uncle Stevie insisted I learn on a manual transmission in case I was ever stuck in a country where they don't have automatic transmissions, which is apparently every country except my own.

"Good," he says. "I'll take over when we get near to Paris. I want to make a list of questions I'll ask the demonstrators and les poulets."

"You're going to interview some chickens?" I ask.

"It's slang. You call them pigs. We call them chickens. It's les fuzz," he says and smiles. "It's only an hour or so. Take one of these." He hands me a little white pill. "I had them put a cooler of Evian and wine on the back seat. Take the pill with the Evian and we'll drink the wine on the way back."

"Are you sure this pill won't put me to sleep?"

"Yes, I'm sure. I took one in my suite. I'm tired too. This is très exciting, no?"

Guy gets us out of the chateau grounds in a cloud of dust. He pulls to the side of the road and makes me take the wheel while he fires up his laptop. I open a bottle of Evian and wash down the pill.

I adjust the seat—you can adjust the seat in a Citroën six different ways including up and down. Guy's head is lowered, keying like mad into his laptop. I shut off the engine. Guy stops keying.

"What are you doing, Swan? You don't know how to drive a stick shift, do you?"

"I know how to drive a stick just fine. I need some answers or I'm going to get out of the car and walk back to the chateau."

"What? What? Come on. Yes, I'm crazy about you, alright?"

"It's about the gun. Under the bench. The murder weapon."

"For God's sake, Swan! The chateau is 500 years old. There must be as many weapons buried in the maze as there are dog bones. How do you know it isn't a gun a servant stole to get later when he goes to see his mother? Half the aristocrat babies in the Loire Valley were conceived in mazes. There are dozens, maybe hundreds, of jealous husbands lying in wait in a maze to catch their wives with their best friend. More importantly, you have to leave the solving of the crime to the gendarmerie. What do you think it would do to French pride if some pretty American divorce avocate just off the airplane solves a crime that they couldn't?

"Hmm."

"Now can we get moving?"

I put the Citroën in gear. "Where are we going, Guy?"

"To Paris," he says. "*Naturellement.*"

"I don't know how to get there."

"Just drive. There are signs all over the place for the autoroute to Paris. In France, all roads lead to Paris."

I pull onto the road and drive and soon I'm on the autoroute to Paris. I'm going very fast and enjoying it, the Citroën rides like a limo, but am still getting buzzed by speeding cars with German and Italian plates.

I drive for about an hour until we approach the outskirts of Paris and he tells me to go on E15, the road that circles Paris. I pull over to let Guy take the wheel. There are a lot of police cars on the shoulder of the road.

"Why are the police out here? The demonstration is in Uncle Stevie and Joe's neighborhood."

"Reinforcements, I guess. In case things get out of hand. Anyway, it's very close. We're practically there."

"What do we do if we get gassed?" I ask.

"We're not going to get gassed," he says.

We pass a cluster of poulets in riot gear.

"Merde. Maybe we are."

He inches the Citroën slowly into narrow streets. A gendarme signals us to pull over to the curb and signs Guy to roll down his window. He asks rapid questions which Guy answers with a disdain unthinkable in America.

"You could never talk to a policeman in America like that," I tell him after the gendarme, satisfied we aren't food terrorists, waves us on. "They'd arrest you."

"Gendarmes expect us to talk to them like that. They expect their fellow countrymen to have a healthy disrespect for authority. Look, there's a space. I think we should park and walk the rest of the way in."

Despite all my experience parking in Boston, I am amazed that Guy manages to squeeze the Citroën into a space between a Fiat and an Audi clearly intended for a car half its size. Both his front and rear tires are up on the curb. I am going to point this out to him but I notice that all the other cars are well onto the sidewalk.

Guy is already running down the street ahead of me, waving his hand for me to stay with him. Within a block we're being carried along by a crush of people carrying signs and wearing pig masks. On their signs are crudely drawn pictures of owls, the symbol of the Athena Corporation with red lines drawn through them. They are chanting in French, which Guy thoughtfully tells me means, "Death to the Franken-Pig. They mean you," he says. "Not you in particular. Americans in general. I've got to get to a café so I can write. Come on."

We veer into a side street and get to a bistro just as a man is getting up from his seat and Guy hip checks an older woman out of the way and takes it. He starts keying into his laptop.

"I'll be five minutes. Don't go any further than the corner or you'll get swept away." He points to the main boulevard we've just left. "Stay right by that street lamp, okay?"

I walk to the corner and stand under the street lamp. So many people of so many ages, not just kids. Wow, this American Frankenfood issue has really hit a French nerve. I am jostled by a student rushing by. The streets are paved with cobblestones, which make walking in my five inch Jimmy Choo heels a challenge. I stagger a little then I slip when another protestor shoves me on his way past. "Hey, watch it!" I yell but I am swept into the flow of the crowd and I can't get back to the safety of the street lamp or move in any direction. I am part of a giant organism that moves me along, my feet barely touching the street. I try to look back for the name of the street where Guy is but I can't. I'm lost. The crowd moves like a giant caterpillar: left then right, left then right. It's the maze all over again. The caterpillar turns right into a giant plaza. Protestors crowd around a raised platform in the middle of the plaza, chanting and thrusting their signs in the air. Finally, one of the protestors wearing a pig mask hops on the platform and yells into a megaphone until the crowd is silenced. I hop up trying to see better as the MC introduces someone and the crowd thunders its appreciation.

Something pokes me in the back. "Hey!" I say, turning to see, to my immense relief, Uncle Joe and Uncle Stevie. "God, am I glad to see you!" I say. "I thought you were going to be watching from your window?"

"I thought we told you not to come," Uncle Stevie says. "We planned to join the demonstration. We knew we might get separated."

"Maybe even arrested," Uncle Joe adds. "Très exciting, no?"

"You've become very French. I don't want French uncles."

"We're opening a restaurant in Paris," Uncle Stevie says. "We need to blend in. Get the lay of the land. Get a feel for things. They're passionate about their food. We want them to know Le Haut Dog shares their passion."

"And their prejudices," Uncle Joe says. "They don't want imported genetically modified food. Especially wheat. They claim you can't make a decent croissant with American wheat. Fine with us. We're making all our buns out of French grains only."

"When did you become so knowledgeable about all this?" I ask. Were these the same uncles who bought hot dog rolls by the truckload in Boston? I never heard a discussion the entire time I was growing up about the origin of the buns. Although I heard plenty of discussion about the cost of those buns.

"My consciousness has been expanded," Uncle Stevie says.

"Mine too. I mean we live here, Swanson. And we're in the food business. Our clients care about where our food comes from. So do we."

"Plus, our girlfriends are very sensitive about these issues," Uncle Stevie says.

"You have girlfriends? French girlfriends?"

"Mais oui!" Uncle Joe says. "It's the only way to really learn a language."

"Dick is always talking about that, too," I say.

"Where is Dick? Why aren't he and Clarisse here? Michel Meriodoc is a hero to this crowd. In some ways, it's not a bad thing he's dead. I mean, it's terrible he's dead, of course, but now the opposition to importing genetically modified food has a saint."

"Well," I say, "There probably more to this than meets the eye."

"Always is," Uncle Joe says.

The crowd, including us, has finally simmered down and the main speaker, wearing the ubiquitous pig mask, takes the stage, to cheering and people stamping their sign poles on the street. The speaker puts his arms out in a sign of victory to even more cheering and when I thought my eardrums were going to explode, he pulls off his mask and there he is: Sébastien Meriodoc

Chapter 22

The Little Dictator

"This should be good," Uncle Stevie says.

"You know him?" I ask. "Hey, watch it," I say to a protestor who pushes me, trying to get closer to the stage.

"I know of him. He is the patron saint of terroir gastronomie."

Terroir gastronomie. There's that phrase again. "What's so special about local cuisine? We're living in a global economy. You can get peaches in January and cherries at Christmas. Personally, I like that."

"But in France, terroir gastronomie is part of their culture. It's making food, growing food like they've always done it in each region. It's like their national art form," Uncle Stevie says.

"Yeah, so how are you contributing to that? With Le Haut Dog?"

"Are you kidding?' Uncle Joe says. "Le Haut Dog is going to encapsulate terroir gastronomie American! You can't get more authentic than that."

"We wouldn't dare compete with the French on their own turf," Uncle Stevie says. "Any more than they would dare compete with us."

"Hot dogs?" I ask.

"Yeah," Uncle Joe says. "Hot dogs."

"With all the junk they grind up to make hot dogs?" I ask.

"That's what makes them authentic, Swanson," Uncle Joe says.

"With the secret Swanson sauce," Uncle Stevie adds.

The sauce that kept them feuding for ten years in Boston. It's not a thing I would like to see resurrected.

"No one can teach you how to make a great hot dog if you haven't spent years in training."

"Yeah, who's that writer that says you have to practice something for 10,000 hours before you're good enough to go pro?" Uncle Stevie asks.

"You mean Malcolm Gladwell?"

"That's the guy! You think Gladwell could make a decent hot dog? He would be the first to admit he couldn't. Ten thousand hours, babe. It takes ten thousand hours."

"He would bow to us professionals. We are the hot dog kings. The best in France."

I have to agree with my uncles cracked logic. They are the hot dog kings. I just don't know if anyone in France would ever bow to them.

The crowd has finally quieted down and Sébastien takes the bullhorn. But naturellement I can't understand what he's saying because he's speaking in French.

"What's he saying, what's he saying?" I tug on Uncle Joe's shirt.

"He's saying that France has a right to maintain its heritage. To its terroir."

"Terroir Francais Toujours! Terroir Francais Toujours!" Sébastien shouts and the people crowded around us take up the chant and Uncle Stevie and Joe join the chanting and Uncle Joe nudges me in the ribs until I join in.

From behind him a man in a pig mask hands Sébastien a large object draped with a black sheet. Sébastien holds it toward the crowd. The man who handed it to him yanks the sheet off. It's a ceramic owl with an American flag painted across its breast. Sébastien holds it above his head for a moment then drops it and it smashes on the podium. He cups a hand to his ear and the volume of the chanting doubles, bouncing off the walls of the surrounding buildings. I stick my fingers in my ears.

Sébastien waves for the crowd to be silent and he starts speaking slowly, calmly, then switches gears. His voice rises an octave, and the passion of what he is saying, though I can't understand a word, I feel moved by it.

A collective gasp goes up.

"Sacre blooey," Uncle Joe says. "He's calling on the dock workers to burn the containers of American seeds that have landed at Le Havre. He's saying that Athena shipped them the minute news of Michel Meriodoc's death came out, that Athena is behind Michel Meriodoc's murder even if they didn't pull the trigger."

A bearded man next to me raises his sign in the air. "*Pas de Frankenfood! Pas de Frankenfood!*" he shouts and starts making a snorting noise, which I realize is supposed to be an "oink" and soon the whole plaza is vibrating with oinking.

"Let's get out of here," Uncle Joe says, pulling me back through the crowd until we're out of the street on the sidewalk.

"I want to try to find Guy," I say.

"You know our address," Uncle Joe says. "Come to our apartment when you find him."

Uncle Joe and Uncle Stevie muscle their way along the sidewalk and disappear into the entrance to a building. For a moment I think "to hell with Guy" and start toward the entryway they disappeared into but then I remember that I have Guy's car keys. He tossed them to me when we got out of the Citroën. I work my way against the flow of people still converging on the plaza. I round a corner and think I see Guy. He's at the edge of an outdoor café.

"Guy!" I yell.

He looks around but I know he can't see me because even in five-inch Jimmy Choos I'm shorter than most of the swirl around me.

But then I see him clearly. He's stood up on a café table and started chanting: "Burn the seeds, burn the seeds, burn the seeds!" His computer case is strapped over his shoulder and he has a mike attached to the lapel of his jacket, and some of the people near him pick up the chant. A rush of admiration explodes in my heart. He's creating his own live podcast. He's amazing. I stop walking toward him so as not to distract him. I'll just watch until he's done. Someone in the crowd in front of him must be rocking the table he's standing on because Guy sways back and forth then disappears from view. The crowd parts and I recognize Paul-Jean from the Meriodoc chateau. Guy has stood up and they are poking each other in the chest and yelling. They start throwing punches and a gendarme is swinging his Billy club at them and Guy crumbles to the ground.

"Let me through, let me through!" I yell. "*Allez! Allez!*" I kick a woman who doesn't move in the knee. She turns on me in a rage and I feel a blow land on my forehead. I touch it and when I look at my hand it's covered in blood. A poulet shoves me aside, joins the first cop and one of them handcuffs Guy.

"He didn't do anything!" I yell.

I run toward Guy and someone pushes me from behind and I trip and fall into the back of the gendarme who's cuffed him. He spins, points at me, and my arms are yanked behind my back and my wrists are snapped into handcuffs.

Chapter 23

Where Are You, Little Star?

I noticed when I was talking on the phone to my uncles from Boston that Parisian sirens wail a lot differently than American sirens which have a nasal squeal like *wnahh wnahh wnahh*. Parisian sirens go too doo too doo and it's kind of a comforting sound, insistent but low decibel. Help is on the way!

Too doo too doo.

Well, let me clarify here that in the back of a French paddy wagon with a bunch of angry food kooks on my way to a French jail it doesn't sound so comforting.

"*Vous êtes une journaliste?*" a young man asks me.

"I don't speak French," I say in my slowest clearest English.

"*Bouf. Une américaine,*" he scoffs to his comrades and laughs, pointing at me.

Now that I really look at them, everyone in the paddy wagon seems ragged and poorly dressed and awfully thin. They look too old to be students, but Uncle Stevie told me in one of our long phone conversations that students in Paris start college at the same age American students are when they're in their junior year.

"What are you doing here, Miss America?" the man asks.

"My boyfriend is Guy de Guy. He's doing a live podcast about the demonstration."

As soon as I say it, of course, I know it was stupid. Guy isn't my boyfriend. We had one real kiss. Okay, five if you count kisses on the forehead and cheeks. But Frenchmen do that with everyone, even their mothers, so they probably don't count.

"Guy de Guy is your boyfriend?" a female student asks me.

"I don't know what you would call it in France. We travel together."

"So what are you, Miss America?" the female student asks. "His secretary?"

See, here's the thing: I have nothing against secretaries. I love secretaries! I've been saving up for one for years but always seem to find something fabulous that I have to raid my secretary savings account to buy. My uncles didn't put me through 4 years of college and 2 years of law school to have people treat me like I key other people's ideas into a computer.

"I'm an attorney," I say in my best courtroom voice.

"An *avocate?*" she says.

I nod yes and the students' expressions change from disdain to respect. Guy was right, the French treat lawyers with deference. I adjust my sensible blouse and navy skirt and put my Jimmy Choo-ed foot out for inspection. "*Trés* expensive," I say. "The fruit of my fees." I smile sweetly.

"*Bouf,*" she says, looking at her fellow protesters as the too doo too doo stops, the engine cuts off, and a gendarme opens the door and gestures for us to get out.

Chapter 24

All Cooped Up

I almost fall when I jump down onto the cobblestones. The gendarme graciously cups my elbow till I regain my balance. "*Merci, beaucoup!*" I say in my best accent and he nods his head imperceptibly. Remind me why I don't like the French again? I think, smiling at him. Oh, yeah, they hit me over the head and arrested me.

The gendarme segregates us into male and female prisoners. Women are shepherded to the left, men to the right, through two separate doors in the back of the police station. I am reminded of a painting I saw in Art History class at Tufts. Handcuffed prisoners circling a yard. A Van Gogh, I think. Considering I have no idea how I'm going to get out of this mess it's not so strange that it popped into my head.

There is a lone woman officer processing all of us. Since I am next to last in line, I crane my neck to watch so my lack of French doesn't give her too much trouble. I know from my association with the law in America that you don't want to piss off the person who has the key to your jail cell.

Another policewoman comes out from behind a desk, frisks the first three women one at a time and stows their wallets etcetera in plastic baggies, then leads them away through a giant metal door. The woman ahead of me in line who is the student who was giving me a hard time in the paddy wagon, flips open her wallet haughtily. The officer looks at her identity card, hands it back to her, whispers something to the processor who tears up her information sheet and gestures to a policeman who escorts her past me. She shoots me a smug look on her way out the door.

"What just happened?" I ask the student behind me.

She sneers. "She is the daughter of the prime minister."

"No kidding? It works that way in France, too?"

"It works that way everywhere, Madame Avocate."

The policewoman beckons me to the desk. "*Vos papiers*," she says.

"I. Do. Not. Speak. French," I say in my slowest English.

She puts her pen down and looks at me for the first time. "*Americaine?*"

I nod.

"*Bouf!*" she says, pushing the intercom button and having a lively discussion I can't understand with someone on the other end. "*Votre passeport?*"

This I understand. "It's in my suitcase. Which is in the chateau I am staying at in Orleans. With the Meriodocs." The Madame Avocate in me kicks in too late and I realize I already said too much. "I would like to speak to the American Consulate," I say.

"Yes, of course, sit over there." She points to a narrow board on metal legs, which is supposed to be a bench.

The other policewoman frisks me and takes away my cell phone, my one link to my uncles and Guy. I hobble over to the bench, plopping myself down. The bench feels oddly comfortable. Even a cactus would at this point because I haven't slept in forty-eight hours. I let my eyelids drop over my eyes. It's like pulling my bedroom shades down and it's suddenly dark and I'm feeling mighty comfy when I hear, "Madame américaine?"

The shades snap up.

"Yes?"

"You must come with me," the policewoman says.

I imagine I am being led to an interrogation room like on CSI, but instead we enter a hallway with cells on either side and she opens the door to a cage which is already filled with twelve other women. Most are sitting on the floor, their legs bent, heads and hands resting on their knees. One woman is leaning against the cage door, staring moodily through the bars. The policewoman gives me a nudge and slams the gate behind me.

I nod to the woman who is standing. She stares back at me with fish eyes. A few of the others check me out then look down again, clearly uninterested. Most of them, although they vary in age from 18 to 45 or 50. are wearing tight thigh high skirts and dangerously high heels and it dawns on me that they are prostitutes. Of course, what else? You can't rob banks in those shoes. My own dangerously high heels feel uncomfortably tight.

"Don't you get a phone call or anything?" I ask no one and everyone. No one chooses to answer me. They are a tribe that can't be bothered acknowledging an outsider's existence.

I realize that the woman I thought was sitting on a chair in the corner is actually sitting on a porcelain toilet. Two women sitting on the floor are talking softly to one another and not in French. It's Arabic. I recognize it from Boston. Algerians, I think.

The policewoman who escorted me returns with the student who was in line behind me. She unlocks the gate and shoves her in. She sniggers when she sees me. "Madame Avocate!" She glances around the cell, decides she and I are from the same tribe and positions herself next to me.

I'm 30 years old but everyone has been calling me madame since I got here. At the chateau I was mademoiselle, a technicality I'll take up with Guy when I get out of here.

"How come you can't get yourself out of this?" she asks me.

"I'm an American lawyer."

"*Ah, oui.*"

A male policeman comes down the hallway with a young man in black leather pants and what we'd call in Boston a guinea tee. He hangs back smoking a cigarette while a woman on the floor who is wearing turquoise hose and matching heels gets up and moves wordlessly toward the gate. The student and I move out of her way and she escapes into the dark hallway with the cop and her pimp.

"I thought prostitution was legal in France," I say.

"It is," the student says, "But a lot of activities associated with it are illegal. Like advertising your goodies or soliciting in a public place known for prostitution or teaching other girls how to be prostitutes. Or wearing suggestive clothes."

"So it's illegal to be a prostitute in France," I say.

"*Vraiment,*" she laughs. I'm surprised she knows so much

about the law and we finally introduce ourselves—her name is Odette—and it turns out she is in the final six months of a course in Centre Régional de Formation to obtain her Certificat d'aptitude à lá profession d'avocate or CAPA. She wants to be a lawyer.

"So get us out of here," I say.

Suddenly I feel something hard hit me on the butt. I turn around and pick up a fushia colored heel. "Hey!" I say, "What's your problem?"

The owner of the shoe says something in French and Odette answers her. She takes off her other shoe and hits Odette in the head.

"*Merde*," Odette says.

"What's going on?" I ask.

"*Bouf!* She asked what we are in here for and I told her we were protesting the importation of Frankenfood. She says that if we had Frankenfood maybe food would be cheaper for people like her and she wouldn't have to walk the streets to feed her kids."

The shoeless woman talks rapidly to the other women who get off the floor, take off their shoes one at a time and start pelting us with them.

"Jeez," I say, covering my head. I seem to be the prime target of the assault.

"I told them you are American," Odette says.

"So?"

"The French blame Americans for everything."

The women close around me in a circle. They start pushing me back and forth from one of them to another.

"You take those four," I command Odette. "I'll take the rest."

"I can't fight," Odette says. "If I have violence on my police record I won't be awarded my CAPA."

"You're kidding right?"

Odette goes limp on the floor and covers her head. So much for *fraternité*.

I crouch in a football stance I'd seen at Patriot pre-season workouts called bull in a ring: knees bent, head tucked into shoulders, arms locked in front of my chest. I turn in a tight circle waiting for someone to strike out at me. I am rushed by a woman who is even shorter than I am—oh, wait, she already threw her shoes at me so that knocked off five inches. I thrust my locked arms into her nose and she crashes down. The next woman comes at me bent over, going for my knees. I step out of her way and blam my locked arms into the back of her neck and push her to the edge of the circle.

"Who do you babes think you're screwing with?" I yell. "I'm from South Boston!"

The adrenaline is coursing through my body and I beckon the next woman to come and get it and when she does I grab the ends of her blond rasta do and twist them while she pummels my head and suddenly I am holding a handful of hair extensions and she screams and grabs the extensions back and goes to a corner crying. I don't blame her, do you know how much those extensions cost?

Two women come at me, one from the front and one from behind, and this time they knock me off balance and I am on the floor and the other women are looking down at me and circling like a pack of wild jackals. Are their eyes really red? I still have my shoes on and I kick and thrust my feet at their shins, landing some pretty sharp hits. But someone behind me is pulling my hair. "Hey, that's not a wig!" I scream. "That's my real hair!" As my hair is being pulled, my ears are being twisted and I'm trying to kick my way out of the circle, I see that Odette has scooched over to the bars and is dragging a shoe back and forth across them making a hellish racket. Someone grabs my foot in mid-kick and snatches off my shoe, then someone tackles my other foot and takes that shoe off too and they use them to pummel me on the shoulders and chest. I cover my face with my arms and think how ironic it is that my obit will say that my shoes are what finally killed me, and not in the way my doctor predicted. I keep kicking blindly even though I know my size 6 ½ feet without Jimmy Choo spike and armor basically inflict no damage whatsoever.

I make myself go deadly still and hold my breath and in that brief pause when my opponents think I might actually be unconscious I let out a Southie fighting yell, jump up and start swinging, landing a few good blows to some breast enhancements when the cell door clangs open and three policemen in full anti-terrorist regalia wade into the cell followed by, who else, Dick.

Chapter 25

Don't Mess With Southie Girls

I brush myself off—Yuck! there's dry blood on my skirt and my blouse is soaked with sweat—and I pat down my hair and feel the giant lump where the gendarme hit me. I snap my fingers for my shoes and balance myself while I put them on deliberately looking each woman in the eye. When I'm ready, the riot police lead me out of the cell. Odette is holding on to the bars, peering out at me, looking scared.

"Thanks for nothing," I say and sashay down the corridor with my escort.

When we get to the front desk, the riot cops disperse and Dick and I face the policewoman behind the tall desk. She looks down at me and sweeps her index finger in a huge arc, stopping at the door.

I don't believe in waiting for verified permission, so I just start walking towards the exit hoping Dick is right behind me. I hear him say something to the desk sergeant in French and they both laugh and then I hear his cleats on the linoleum floor. I go outside and am shocked by the beautiful September weather: hot sun, cool air. It's amazing how even a little time in jail will make you appreciate your freedom. I breathe it all in deeply, grateful for whatever force led Dick to me in this jail.

When I feel his presence behind me, I say, "What took you so long, Dick? Those women were tearing me apart."

"It looked like you were holding your own," he says.

"It was twelve to one. I'm a humble blue-collar divorce lawyer from Boston. I'm not an action hero."

"You're from Southie, aren't you?" Dick says. "I wasn't worried at all. Southie chicks are tough."

Only a complete dinosaur like Dick would call a woman a chick. And get away with it.

"Aren't you going to ask me how I found out where you were?"

That's the thing about Dick: he is so proud of his skill that he can often lose track of the human side of the hunt, in this case, me.

"Okay, Dick, how did you find out where I was? How did you even know I was gone?"

"The desk sergeant answered your cell phone. I called about 20 times. She finally picked up." He looked mighty pleased with himself. He pulls my cell phone out of his pocket and hands it to me with my passport. "Oh," he says, "And you might want to carry this with you in France. Everyone in Europe carries identification papers. I found it in your luggage."

"My suitcase is locked," I say.

"You know what they say about locks," he says.

Right. Locks only keep out honest people. Dick's favorite rule.

"Why did you even call me?"

"I went up to the chateau when I finished doing yoga and Tulane told me you had just left for Paris with Guy. She said your uncles had called and warned you not to come so I called them. They said you'd gone looking for Guy in the middle of a riot. I tried Guy's cell phone. No answer. So I called a contact of mine in the Paris gendarmerie, he said they had an American girl without any ID—I thought you should know he called you a girl—locked up in a holding cell, and voilà, you're welcome.

Dick leads me to his car. The shock of being in a riot and being in jail is starting to subside and I remember that I have something very important to tell Dick: I found the murder weapon that was used to kill Meriodoc in the maze behind the chateau.

"What I'd like to know is what you did to get those ladies so worked up," Dick says.

"In the cell? You think that rumble was my fault?"

"They weren't beating up that other woman."

"She was a wuss."

"She also didn't get her clothes messed up or her eye blackened."

"My eye is black?"

"It's going to be."

"They found out we…"

"We?"

"Me and that wuss. Her name is Odette. She's on the last leg of getting her certificate to practice law and she said she wouldn't get it if she helped me fight. She told them we were in the protest against importing Frankenfood."

"Were you?"

"Yes, of course. Where did you think I was?"

"I thought you were helping me find Meriodoc's murderer like you promised."

"Well, I do have some news on that front. In fact, I basically solved the murder for you while you were doing your morning yoga exercises."

"What? Who?"

"Well, I don't know who yet, but that's just a technicality. Once you take finger prints from the murder weapon, *voilà!*"

"You found the murder weapon?"

"Yes." I was feeling pretty good about myself. I had fended off a cell full of crazed prostitutes and solved a nationally perplexing murder. Maybe now everyone would let me get some sleep.

"What did you do with it, Swanson?"

"I didn't do anything with it. I left it there."

"Where?"

"In the maze."

"You found it in the maze? Was it just tossed there? How do you know it was the murder weapon? The chateau is used for hunting. There's no official count of all the guns there."

Which was just what the garage guy said. "It was buried. Under a bench. Devil Dog found it actually."

"And you just left it there?"

"I was going to tell you but Guy and I left in a hurry for Paris." Which was a half-truth, of course. I let Guy talk me out of it. He had to "take care of things" he said.

"Now the murder weapon, if it is the murder weapon for this

particular murder is hopelessly polluted."

Dick's Rule One: Once people get their grubby little paws on evidence, all hope of solving a crime is lost in a smudgy swamp of fingerprints.

"I have to see my uncles," I say.

"We don't have time," Dick says. "You can see them when we find Meriodoc's murderer."

Discussion over. We drive to a main drag and follow the signs out of Paris toward Orleans.

Chapter 26

One Lump? Or Two?

Besides the five outbuildings including two hunting lodges, the Chateau Meriodoc has 13 guest bedrooms, 5 suites for family, and an entire wing for servants, of which there used to be many. Tulane and her father, Theodore, are in charge of a small army of people in old fashioned uniforms dusting and polishing, clipping and mowing, shining and buffing, washing and ironing.

"Most of them are from the village, they don't live here," Tulane tells me. She makes me a big pot of tea which I drink with honey and milk. Lots of honey. "They are kind of like, what do you call them in America? Temps?"

"That's what we call them." I bite into a croissant left over from breakfast.

"It's better with this," Tulane says, pushing a jar of strawberry jam towards me.

I load up the croissant with the dense red goo and dig in. "Yes, it is," I say.

Dick has run to the hunting lodge to make sure Clarisse is okay. He told me to wait for 15 minutes and we would go into the maze and find the hunting rifle that Devil Dog dug up.

I am sitting at the big kitchen table the servants eat their meals at. Devil Dog barely barks hello to me, but then his ear is wrapped in gauze where Hannibal tore it and Tulane tells me that the vet gave him a heavy sedative because he needed 20 stitches to close all the wounds Hannibal dug with his talons. Still? Not even a flicker of affection? His eyes follow Tulane around like a lovelorn

112

puppy's. He seems to have a thing for European women. He was completely smitten with Ulrike Meiner, the S&M babe in my last divorce case. Who knows what his life was like before my uncles adopted him for me?

Tulane sits across from me. "He will be more alert in a few hours. Dachshunds are very hearty animals. Even with stitches, he'll be up and around."

I can see now that she is pregnant. When she leans back to make her baby comfy I see a little bump.

"What's it like?" she asks, leaning her elbow on the table.

I take another bite of jam sweetened croissant. "Scrumptious!"

"Not the croissant! I mean, what's it like being in jail?"

"Oh, that." News travels fast. "One toilet."

"How many do you need?"

"I mean one toilet for 14 women. We were all crammed in a cell with one toilet, which some woman was using for a chair, and one sink which didn't look like anybody had ever used."

She looks at me dreamily. "I always wondered what it would be like."

"I don't think," I say, "it actually was a jail. I think it was where they hold people until they charge them and take them to prison or release them. It was mostly prostitutes."

" Just prostitutes? No murderers?"

"Not that I know of. I mean, it wasn't a chatty bunch. I think they thought we were the most dangerous people there."

"We?"

"Odette and me. She's a law student. We were both at the protest. The other women in the cage thought that GMO food was a good idea, that high-yield food would be cheaper and they might be able to afford food without supplementing their income by turning tricks."

"*Bowf.*"

"*Bowf,* indeed."

"But no murderers, really?"

I shove the last piece of croissant in my mouth and wash it down with tea. A book is open face down on the table in front of Tulane. It's "Dead Wrong" by my fabulous friend Bathsheba Monk who wrote about my adventures with the Bledsoe family. It was an instant bestseller and translated into 5 languages, but it's still surprising to see it here in a chateau in the middle of France.

"You know," I say, pointing to the book. "You can't take all the stuff Bathsheba writes at face value. She makes being a murderer sound glamorous. But it isn't. I mean, someone dies. That's the one move you can't take back."

"Yes, but the murderer in here," she taps the book, "Does something about what she sees as an injustice to her family. I admire that. Taking action. You can't wait for people to decide to respect you. You have to demand their respect." Tulane's eyes glow and a film of sweat appears on her forehead and cheeks.

She pours fresh tea into my cup but suddenly I'm not thirsty because of the very real possibility that I am taking tea with Michel Meriodoc's murderess. I slowly push the cup toward Tulane and move my chair back from the table in case she goes mad and attacks me. "Is there something you want to tell me, Tulane?"

She looks at me quizzically. "Tell you? Oh! You think I am the murderer." She laughs. "Why would I kill the father of my child? Michel was going to give us the farm, you know? Where Sébastien lives."

Theodore told Guy and me that Meriodoc thought he was better than him which meant Tulane wasn't good enough for him either.

"He told you that?"

"Not in so many words," she says.

"How many words then?" I ask.

"He loved me. That's three words!" She puts up three fingers and laughs. "I've known him since I was a little girl. I was born here. Me and my father sort of come with the property, you know? We're like serfs. I mean, we could leave, yes, but then what are you suited for? It's an unjust system."

I nod.

"Well, Michel wanted to change that."

"Did he?"

"Yes! A bequest was in his will that we get the farm when he died."

"He wanted to wait until he died?"

"He was a very progressive man. Look at what he wanted to do about genetically modified food. He wanted to ban it."

"Some people would say he was the exact opposite of

progressive. That opposing genetically modified food is stopping progress."

"Doesn't matter. Look, Swanson, I don't think he really loved me. He loved the idea of me. The idea that he could live his life au terroir, the idea that people could live their entire life and have all their needs met within a ten mile radius. That was me! What better lover than a girl who grew up on the family's estate?"

"Is that why he and Clarisse were divorcing?"

"Clarisse is very beautiful, very *sophistiquée*. Michel was smitten with her. That's not so hard to believe."

Tulane, while an attractive girl, is certainly not the great beauty that Clarisse is. But it doesn't seem to bother her.

"But what did Clarisse see in him? She's like 40 years younger than him."

"That's not so unusual in France," Tulane says.

"It doesn't seem to me that she ever loved him. She doesn't hate him enough now for dying, you know what I mean?"

"Maybe you should ask Bill Barnum about that."

"Clarisse's father? Why him?"

"Servants are like hidden cameras in a big estate like this," Tulane says. "Eyes everywhere." She makes circles out of her fingers and looks through them and laughs. "You are invisible, part of the landscape. You would be astonished at what servants know."

"Why don't you tell me what you know?" I ask.

"Because, I am paid to be discreet."

"That's all?"

"Plus it won't bring Michel back, will it? There's a big difference between the French and the Americans. The French despise authority because every last French man thinks he knows more than the authorities and so he withholds pieces of information because he thinks, 'why should I help you do your job? You should find what you want to know on your own without me giving you clues'."

"You mean me, don't you?"

"*Oui*. You will find out what you need to know when the time comes. Then you will piece it all together and make sense out of it and we French will accept it as fact."

"And what do you think Americans are like?" I feel my neck

getting hot.

"Americans find out a little piece of information and think they have the whole truth. Like you think now that I was in love in Michel."

I nod.

"And then you think, because of that, I couldn't have killed him."

I nod again.

"But you know, Swanson, you might be wrong."

She laughs and I don't know what to think when Dick sticks his head in the kitchen door. "Swanson, meet me in the salon, will you?"

Chapter 27

The Stew Thickens

A big cook comes into the kitchen to start preparing the evening's dinner, the main part of which—a leg of lamb—was already stewing on the stove which has eight burners. She takes off her sweater and hangs it on the row of hooks by the door, puts on her floor-length apron and immediately goes to work as if we weren't there, mumbling to herself in French.

"I must work," Tulane says. "Too many have stayed for the hunt tomorrow."

"The hunt?" I exclaim. "They're going to hunt something here tomorrow?"

"It is a hunting lodge," she reminds me.

"Come on, Devil Dog," I order him. Devil Dog looks from Tulane to me and I finally pick him up and carry him upstairs. "You're pathetic," I tell him. "One look from a French girl and you're gonzo." He's still woozy from the pain medication and doesn't flinch when I hug him.

We reconvene in the salon, which is next to the library where Meriodoc was laid out. Jeezums, was it just last evening? It seems like a month ago. I put Devil Dog down. He hobbles to the open doorway, whimpers, and goes into hiding behind the drapes. His encounter with Hannibal has obviously spooked my brave boy.

The drapes are drawn so the room is dark, but I can see that seating and side tables have been arranged around a round table with a gorgeous display of hybrid yellow day lilies and purple hosta flowers in a silver vase in the middle.

Farewell, Meriodoc. Don't let the door hit you on the way out.

Dick opens the curtains on one of the windows and in the light a woman takes form on a love seat in the corner.

"Sylvie!" I cry.

"Hello Swanson," she says. "I hear you got yourself into a bit of a jam this morning. There is a rule in demonstrations. You never run towards the police, you run away from them."

"Your husband was there. He was the main event, in fact."

I notice that she didn't bother covering up her shiner with make-up. We are *en famille* apparently and don't have to dress up for one another.

"He is good at throwing smoke in people's face. He wants GMO seeds. Believe me!"

"He called on the students to burn the seeds from the Athena Corporation on the docks."

"Of course," Sylvie says. "He will get the French in such a fury against American GMO seeds they will jump at the opportunity to have French GMO seeds. He is talking to Athena now about creating a French branch."

"What about Bill Barnum? Isn't he supposed to be bringing Athena to France?"

"He is working with Sébastien. Clarisse too. They were going to gang up on Michel about French GMOs till he relented."

"But it didn't work," I say.

"Don't worry," Sylvie says, "No one's going to be burning anything. The seeds will never make it off the freighters."

"How can you be so sure?"

"Because Guy will make sure they won't."

"You know Guy?"

She gives me an incredulous look. "Of course I know Guy. He's my brother."

I let that tidbit of information sink in for a minute then I say, "Right. Of course. Your brother. I knew that." Guy told me was he was going to help his sister who was in an abusive relationship. It never occurred to me that his sister might be Sébastien's wife. Although, the description he gave me matches their marriage.

Dick was busying himself with the curtains. "Damn!" he says to no one in particular. "This cord arrangement is confusing."

I want him to ask Sylvie some questions, but Dick-in-love isn't the Dick I know. He's been in a fog since I met him for lunch in Boston. No wonder he wanted me to come to France and help him. He's probably resisted falling in love the whole time I've known him because love saps his ability to think. I clear my throat to get his attention. He continues to toy with the curtains.

"Are you and Sébastien getting divorced?" I ask Sylvie.

"Why would I divorce him now that we're going to cash in?" she asks.

"Because, he did that?" I point to her black eye.

"Oh yes, my eye," she says and purses her lips. "I walked into a door, you know?"

As a frugal shopper I know the value of things. I mean, I would never pay full price for a pair of Jimmy Choos even if I have to wait until they've cooled off from their debut on the runway, because then you are just paying for the thrill of the hunt, for being the first to have them. Give it a couple of months and the shoe is demoted to being just a shoe. And I say that as a complete shoe-a-holic. So, if I know the value of things, what's the price of a fortune? A bitter life where you stop loving your husband because he isn't giving you what the people in the next house have? A life where painting out black eyes with Cover Girl is part of your daily skin-care routine?

"You know your inheritance isn't what you thought it was going to be? Now that Tulane is pregnant with Meriodoc's child, you're percentage has gone down."

Sylvie laughs. "Who cares about that? We'll be going to market with French GMO seeds within the month and we'll be rich in our own right."

Before I can answer Sylvie, a door opens and Clarisse comes into the salon wrapped in a black cashmere shawl which accentuates her pale beauty. Piaf and Chocolat are at her side, toe nails clicking on the marble floor. Devil Dog comes out from behind the drapes and the dogs do a round of sniffing then they all rush out of the room, Devil Dog whimpering as he runs. It occurs to me that Devil Dog could get used to living here. That he might think he was the poodles equal and not just a diversion. I think of Guy.

Dick rushes over to Clarisse.

"Darling, you should be resting!" he says to her.

Why wasn't he concerned with my beauty sleep? I haven't been in a bed for two days.

"And what have you had to eat all day?" he demands.

And what have I had to eat? Tea and croissants. Where was Guy, anyway? Clarisse murmurs something, and he pulls at one of the chords that alert a servant to come. A maid hurries in and listens as Dick specifies what snack he wants brought *"immédiatment! Vous comprenez!"* for his beloved who eases down on the love seat next to Sylvie, her little velvet ballet slippers peeking out from beneath her long black skirt. She is the very model of elegant mourning.

"I'm so proud of Sébastien," Clarisse says. "He's carrying on Michel's tradition. Asking the students to burn the GMO seeds. It's radical, but effective I think."

"What about your father?" Sylvie asks, smirking. "Aren't you concerned about him? Isn't his career dependent on bringing in the French contract for Athena?"

Clarisse puts her hand on Sylvie's. "He won't need it now that we have this. He can retire."

"You mean this chateau?" Sylvie withdraws her hand. "It's only yours to sell if no one wants to live here."

"Who would want to sell?" Clarisse asks. "This is the ideal home base. Dad loves to explore. He could ride his bike all around France."

"I would very much like to sell," Sylvie says.

Hey, wait, I think, Back up! First my uncles desert me for France and obviously Dick would follow Clarisse to the ends of the earth. Even Devil Dog loves it here. I can't breathe.

"But surely," Clarisse says, "Sébastien doesn't want to sell. What's he going to do?"

"We're going to move to Paris," Sylvie says. "Paris is the only city worth living in. You know, you only get so many chances to do what you want in life. This may be my last chance to do what I want."

"But what about Sébastien?" Clarisse persists. "His career? He's always worked for his father, perfecting local species. Au terroir is his life. In Paris he wouldn't know what to do with himself. He's a farmer. He must stay here."

"He's not a farmer!" Sylvie says angrily. "And he already has a plan. We have a plan."

"You do? I must say, that's a relief," Clarisse says, looking the exact opposite of relieved. Dick comes up behind her and puts his hand on her shoulder and I notice—or was it my imagination—that she flinches slightly before she reaches up to hold it.

It kind of surprises me that Clarisse is protective of her stepson. But it always surprises me when very beautiful women are concerned about anyone other than themselves. Yes, I know, this is prejudiced. But there it is.

The floor length windows in the salon open out to the balcony. A slight breeze ruffles the sheers that cover them then a bigger wind blows them wide open. A male figure is standing in the window, silhouetted against the setting sun.

"Guy!" Sylvie cries.

"Guy!" I cry.

Guy steps into the room and surveys the scene as if he finds the situation highly amusing. He kisses me first, then Sylvie who all of a sudden can't stop looking at me.

Guy claps his hands and shouts, "I just got out of jail! What does a person have to do to get a drink around here?"

Chapter 28

What Does A Guy Have To Do To Get A Drink Around Here?

Sylvie composes herself enough to ask, "So who sprung you?"

"Jail was wonderful, sis, thank you for asking." Guy finds the drink cart and pours himself a thick glass of scotch, downs the contents, then raises it in my direction. "Darling, may I?"

"I'll have one," Sylvie says.

He pours drinks for everyone, even Clarisse who holds the glass as if it were filled with plutonium. "To our wonderful French judicial system which couldn't think of a good reason to keep me in jail. And to the beautiful Swan," he raises his glass in a toast, "Who joined me on the barricades and paid the price for her convictions by sitting for several hours in a cell with French Algerian prostitutes. And I hear she took them all on. Well done, Swan."

"Yes," Dick says, "To the Swan." He winks at me devilishly and I blush. Everyone raises their glasses to me and drinks. I want to tell Guy that I was arrested only because I was trying to help him. I couldn't bear to see the gendarmes roughing him up, although when I see him now, it doesn't seem that they did much damage. He looks as handsome as when we drove into the city together.

"It wasn't just prostitutes. There was a student in jail with me, too," I say.

"Students are always in jail in Paris," Guy says. "It's part of their education."

"They all knew you," I say.

"Students read blogs. Even lifestyle blogs like mine. It's a diversion from actually studying."

"You're still a hero."

"So, to me!" He raises his glass to the ceiling then comes over with the bottle and refills mine. I smile, remembering our first dinner together when he got me tipsy—no, drunk—on scotch. "So, to you!" I say.

Clarisse hands her untouched glass to Dick who puts it on a coffee table. "I have to go look after my father," she says, wrapping her shawl tightly around her shoulders and leaving, Dick on her trail like a guard dog.

The setting sun is sitting on the balcony railing and its orange light is right on my face, almost blinding me. It's just me and Guy and Sylvie in the salon. Guy pulls a chair opposite me and sits down, his knees touching mine. The warmth from his body makes me giddy. I feel like I'm going to swoon with desire. Just kiss me, dammit! I want to shout at him.

"So, Swan," he says.

"Yes?" I say dreamily.

"Who done it?"

"Who done what?"

"Who killed Meriodoc?"

Sylvie has pulled a chair up next to mine and is looking at me through slitted eyes.

"Well…" God, they're so intense.

"Isn't that why you're here?" he asks.

"I suppose."

"So, what do you think?"

He refills my glass. "What have you found out?"

I want to say something helpful. "Theodore is an angry man," I say. "That garage guy? You know?"

"He's very angry," Guy agrees. "He thinks because he has to work for him he isn't as good as Meriodoc."

"Well, there's more of course."

"Isn't there always," he says.

I want Guy to smile at me. I smile at him to give him the idea. "And Tulane, of course, has a real motive. Meriodoc would never marry her because she's a peasant."

"Tsk, tsk," Guy says. He pulls out a Gauloise and offers me one.

I forget my decade long battle to quit and accept both it and the forthcoming light.

"What about Clarisse?"

"Ah, Clarisse." I drink the glass of scotch and Guy immediately refills it. "She's not very passionate. I can't see her pulling the trigger on someone she is clearly still fond of. Still, she has a motive. She would get more as a widow than a divorcee."

"You already know our laws," Guy says admiringly. "She's very smart," he says to Sylvie.

"And her father, Bill Barnum, benefits greatly of course because Meriodoc was keeping Athena products out of France. Now that he's gone, swoosh!" I make a big circle with my glass. "Let the GMOs flow!"

"He almost seems the most likely, don't you think?" Guy asks.

They all seem suspect to me. I can't see Sylvie's face because she is backlit. Sébastien is a likely candidate because of Tulane's baby, but it seems rude to mention at the moment.

"It's pretty complicated," I say. "And the murder weapon has been polluted."

"Murder weapon?"

"The hunting rifle Devil Dog dug up in the maze. Remember?"

He shakes his head.

"I could have sworn I told you about the rifle after I came out of the maze," I say.

"I don't remember that you found anything. You weren't carrying anything when you came out."

"I'm taking a nap before dinner," Sylvie says, getting up suddenly.

Yes, go," Guy says.

"Are you staying the night here or at the farm?" she asks Guy and leaves without waiting for a reply.

Guy looks at me and smiles sweetly. "Here."

Chapter 29

A House Divided

I let Guy lead me upstairs.

"My room is right next to yours," he says.

"No kidding?" I say.

"I arranged it. Are you mad?"

Was I mad? "So what's the dinner tonight and what's the hunt tomorrow? What's going on?"

"It is a hunting lodge, so, we hunt. You've never hunted before?"

"I live in Boston, Massachusetts," I remind him.

"I live in Boston, Massachusetts, too, remember? We can't hunt there anymore. Too many people." He pretends to shoot a rifle all over the place.

"Right."

We wound our way up the staircase, staring at generations of dead Meriodocs along the way.

"Why didn't you tell me that you knew Meriodoc? And that Sylvie is your sister? I feel like an idiot."

"It's not that I don't trust you…"

"What's to trust me with? It seems weird that you wouldn't mention it."

"I'm sorry, Swan, I really am. I like you, you know. I more than just like you. I didn't want to drag you into our family mess…"

"Well, I'm right in the middle of your family mess now."

"…before you got to know me and like me."

"All families are messes, once you get to know them. No

matter how together they seem on the surface, once you get in, wow. Believe me, I know. All I deal with are families that have stopped functioning. "

Maybe divorce is just the outward sign that a family had stopped functioning. In my short career, I'm always astounded at the anger and resentments that come spilling out once you pull the plug on a marriage.

"Marriage. Family. Both are unnatural if you ask me," Guy says. "Expecting grown people who have nothing more in common than their parents to like each other, much less agree on things."

I always wanted a brother or sister. I always imagined we would be close and sing happy birthday to each other, do things that no one else ever remembers to do without prodding. I never thought it would be a negative thing like Guy was implying.

"Look at Sylvie and me," Guy says. "She is so materialistic. The only reason she married Sébastien was for his money. And now she is full of rage because she thinks Sébastien doesn't want to share it with her and instead of reassuring her he hits her. In France, we have this system that you can't inherit the way you can in America. It's all about the family here. Not about the family's happiness, mind you, but the family keeping control of property. That's the important thing. It goes back to Charlemagne. He divided his kingdom among his sons and the family got weaker and weaker the more things were divided. Now it's impossible to divide a piece of property."

I kind of knew what he was talking about. Uncle Joe and Uncle Stevie hadn't spoken in ten years—dividing the house in half, opening identical hot dog shops across the street from each other in South Boston, taking half the business away from each other. It was only when they joined forces that they seem on the verge of achieving something close to a happy life. Even, I think ruefully, if that happy life is happening across "the pond" in France.

"But I have to help her when she is in trouble, you know?"

We reach my room. "Is she in trouble, Guy?"

"I don't know. All that anger with no place to go. I will have to confront Sébastien if he keeps fighting with Sylvie. But I don't want to do it because Sébastien is my meal ticket at this point. I have an exclusive to write about what he thinks, what he's going to do. That exclusivity is what makes my blog valuable. But Sylvie is my family. We were poor together for a long time, Swan. I can't desert her now."

"I only have my uncles," I say. "They are the only family I have. Without them, who am I?" I ask.

"You have to invent yourself. You have to take what you like from different people and create a life for yourself. That's very American, but I can never say it on my blog."

Deep down in my soul, I know that Uncle Joe and Uncle Stevie would do anything for me, but at the end of the day, I have to make my own life just like they are making theirs. French girlfriends! That's why it's so important to find someone to create a life with. Solo is just too damned lonely. I touch the door handle to my room. "Do you want to come in?" I ask Guy.

"I would like that very much, Swan."

Chapter 30

All You Need Is Love

Sometimes, I think life was easier in the 1940s and 50s when you weren't allowed to have sex before you were married. It was easier because you had nothing to compare it with. You had sex with the man you married and that was your lot in life. Of course, that may be why so many of our grandmothers drank their lunches. They were missing something, but didn't know what exactly. No facebook confessions. No comparison shopping.

Anyway, when Guy comes into my room, I know that I want him even though the memory of my beloved Hidalgo is still parked in the poll position.

"What's that?" I ask. An ice bucket on a stand is by the sofa in my sitting room, a weird bottle that looks like a sculpture made from magenta balloons, a modern take on the ancient fertility goddess, Isis, in the bucket.

"I had Tulane fix us something." He seems embarrassed. "Do you mind?" Little sandwiches with the crusts cut off and cookies are arranged artfully on a tray next to the champagne stand.

"But what's this?" I pick up the weird bottle and read the label: Dom Pérignon rosé champagne. I suppose the balloons look kind of bubbly, though the net effect looks to me like basset hound balls.

"It's a limited edition Jeff Koons designer bottle. Do you like it?"

"Actually, I don't."

"He's not French, he's American."

"I still don't like it."

"Well, as a lifestyle critic, I get all this promotional stuff. If you're going to be with me, you have to get used to cutting edge things and at least try to understand them." He peers at me, as if anxious for my reaction.

"Are we going to be together?" It's all I care about at the moment.

Guy takes me in his arms and kisses my forehead, then my eyes which close to enjoy the sensation of his lips on me, then finally my mouth. I want it to go on forever. He pushes me away and my eyes pop open.

"Do you want that?" he asks.

"Yes, why did you stop?"

"No, I mean, do you want us to be together?"

I nod. I really really really do.

Guy opens the bottle of Dom Pérignon and pours pink champagne into two flutes. We intertwine our arms and lock eyes. "To being together," he says.

"Together."

We drink and Guy takes our flutes and puts them on an end table, takes my hand and leads me to the bedroom. I am really happy for the first time in months. There are two robes in the armoire. Guy throws one to me and we undress shyly and put them on, sneaking glances at one another.

I try to hide myself, but Guy horses around and pulls my robe open, making me dance with him—he pulls me in with one hand then twirls me around and spins me out like he's Fred Astaire and I'm Ginger Rogers—and amazingly we hear the same music and our feet are in step and our bodies create a new ballet.

He feeds me a little sandwich and pours us another glass of pink champagne, then lying next to me in the silk and linen covered bed that looks like a ship that got unmoored from reality and became the vehicle for my fantasy, Guy gathers me close and says the three little words that make any woman bold, the three little words that will make any woman give her heart freely.

Guy leans in and whispers, "You've lost weight."

Chapter 31

The Ugly Duckling Becomes A Swan

It's seven o'clock when I awaken from a dream in which I'm riding on the back of Hannibal through the forest then up into the inky blue sky. I think if I could just reach a little further out I would be able to touch the moon, but instead when I reach out Hannibal banks and I fall off of him, swirling down and down and I'm about to crash into the maze when I sit up, sweating, and breathing hard. It's dark in the room, but I can see the same moon as in my dream through the open window.

I tap around the bed, but it's empty. I hear water running through the old pipes in the next room and the door opens and Guy is standing there, his face covered with shaving cream.

"We have a door that adjoins our rooms," he says and sits on the bed next to me and runs his finger down the side of face and my neck and shoulders. "You okay?"

"Better than okay," I say.

"Me too. You have to get ready for dinner. They start at 8:30. They're having cocktails now."

"Were you downstairs?"

"No, but that's their routine and I've never known it to vary."

Guy goes back into his bathroom to continue shaving. I grab my robe—that was hastily discarded on the floor when our afternoon began—wrap it around me and go to his room, lean against the door jamb and watch him.

"That was nice," I say.

"Very. It could become habit forming."

I smile. I hope it will.

While everything in my suite is shades of green, everything in Guy's suite is done in lapis lazuli blue. The wall paper in his bathroom is that intense shade with Fleur de Lis embossed in gilt. I wander into his bedroom and am startled by its beauty. All blue with gold and black accents. I'll have to put more effort into decorating my apartment in Brookline.

"Do you have something to wear?" he asks, splashing his face with water and toweling off.

"What do you mean, something to wear? Of course I have something to wear."

"I mean, the people here dress for dinner."

It dawns on me what he means. "Something like a dinner gown?" I ask.

"Exactly."

I have two short navy blue skirts and five white blouses. Several pair of L'egg pantyhose in nude. Three pairs of Jimmy Choos in various jewel tones. Five pair of thong panties and three underwire bras in escalating shades of red. That's it. "No," I admit. "Just the usual work stuff."

"People leave stuff sometimes. Let's see what's in the armoires."

We open the armoire in his room first. Stacks of blankets and pillows. Guy's dinner jacket is on the bar alone.

"Let's try your room," he says.

"I haven't even unpacked," I say, thinking everything I own is probably hopelessly wrinkled as well as hopelessly wrong.

We go into my room and open the armoire. Only a tuxedo someone left. I'm crestfallen.

"Nothing," I say.

"What do you mean, nothing!" Guy pulls the tuxedo out of the armoire and holds it up to me. "It's perfect."

"It drags a little," I say.

"Not with your heels on," he says.

"I can't wear a man's tuxedo when all the other women are going to be in formal dresses!" I say. I feel like crying. My first night as Guy's woman and I'm going to be a social flop because I didn't know enough to bring a good dress to France with me. Not that I actually own such a dress.

"Women in men's tuxedos are the sexiest hippest things

around," he says.

"How do you know what's hip for a woman? You're a man."

"I am France's premier lifestyle critic. If it's not chic now it will be after I post your photo wearing it on my blog."

Guy is brushing off the tuxedo and examining the seams, when he looks up at me and says, "Into the shower! Go! Go!"

And I run in and stand under the gently flowing water letting it stream all over me, shampooing my hair, when Guy comes in and says, "Come out! Out! Out!"

I turn off the water. "You are certainly bossy," I say.

I am fluffing my hair up with a towel and he takes the towel from me and says, "Don't comb it, we'll let it dry naturally," which, I don't know if he's aware of this, but naturally in my case means my fine hair will spike out in all directions.

"Whatever."

The tuxedo is laid out on my bed along with my brightest red bra. "You went through my clothes!"

"Hurry up and get into this," he said. "Where's your make-up?"

I pull on my thong and red bra. "If I didn't have empirical evidence to the contrary," I say, "I would bet you were gay."

He laughs. "I am European. American's always think it's not masculine to care about how you look, but I love to look at beautiful women. Beautiful interesting women, like you, Swan. Put on the trousers, s'il vous plâit."

I am surprised at how well they fit, except they are about three inches too long. "Put on the heels, the red ones," he says. "Vite! Vite! And now this," he drapes the jacket over my shoulders. "Come on, push your arms through."

"I need a blouse!" I say. "I can't wear a jacket open to here and not have a blouse on."

"Au contraire," he says, "Believe me, no one will miss the blouse, they will be too busy looking at you." He fluffs my hair with the towel and puts some spray in it, then grabs my make-up case and pulls out just a lipstick, the brightest red I have, a Chanel color called Midnight Red and holds my chin in his hands while he applies it.

"Are you sure you're not gay?" I ask him.

He laughs and kisses me. "What do you think?" Then he turns

me around where I am facing a sexy Euro version of myself in a full length mirror and he says, "Et voilà!"

I gasp.

"You like it?"

"I look so…" I'm trying to find the right word. For one thing, the jacket dips so low you see tons of cleavage, but because of the red bra it doesn't look like I forgot to get dressed, it just makes me look "…interesting," I say. "I look interesting."

"Good, no? So, let's go!"

"Wait," I say, "You have to get dressed!"

"Ah, oui," he says, looking down at his naked body. "I knew that."

He runs back into his room while I continue admiring myself in the mirror. I look good!

"Hey, Guy," I yell into his room. "Mind if I borrow one of your blankets?" It's kind of cold in my bedroom and as I said, my armoire isn't stocked like his is.

"Come in, come in," he yells back. "I'm in the bathroom. Help yourself to whatever you need."

I walk in. I'm not actually used to just coming and going out of men's bedrooms. I'm not that experienced with men period. But the new Euro me is feeling quite confident and I stride into Guy's bedroom and turn on a light by his bed, which hasn't even been ruffled I note with a grin—all the ruffling has been done in my room—and I examine the bedroom with the beautiful blue—a breathtaking carving of a stag being dragged down by a pack of hunting dogs in lapis lazuli is on the center of the mantelpiece flanked by two candlesticks in lapis. I catch sight of myself in the mirror and I like what I see. I feel grown-up and sure of myself. My old Southie self was good when I was young, I think, but this new European sophistication agrees with the thirty-year-old me. I made love with one of the most important cultural critics in France and he gave me a makeover and jeez, just think, I was even in a demonstration and in jail today. How hip and savvy is that! I'm like one of those cool celebrity women who live life to the hilt and on several continents, performing acts of charity for third-world children who fight for the chance to cram into pictures that international journalists take of me for vodka ads. Or shoe ads, not sure. I'm laughing already at the charming anecdotes I will share at the dinner table tonight in my atrocious to non-existent French. They will forgive me because I look so…French!

There's a cold draft coming in, so I cross the room to close the doors that lead to the balcony and hit my leg on a glass coffee table. "Damn!" I bend to rub it when I see a stack of papers on the table. The handwriting on the brown envelope looks familiar. I pick it up then drop it like a hot potato. It's Clarisse's divorce file. The one I forgot on the plane.

Chapter 32

Everything Is Relative

I race out of Guy's bedroom into my own room and slam the door behind me. Without thinking, I grab my purse and run—well, as fast as you can run in 5 inch heels—down the marble staircase and past some guests and out the salon door to find Dick, who is running up the balcony steps, "to find you!" he exclaims out of breath.

We put our hands on each other's shoulders and pant.

"Guy…" I finally get out.

"Clarisse…" he says.

We look at each other and drop our hands.

"Clarisse what?" I ask.

"I did a background check on her."

"You did a background check on someone you want to marry?"

"Swanson, that's the most naïve thing you've ever said. Of course you would do a background check on someone you want to marry. You'd be a fool not to!"

The clouds have disappeared from Dick's eyes. He's no longer in love.

"Is it bad?" I ask.

"Couldn't be worse. Come here." The old take-charge Dick was back. He pulls me down the steps. The salon is completely lit up and people are starting to enter from the sitting room where they were having smokes and drinks. We park ourselves under a salon window where we can watch but not be seen.

"Anything strike you odd about Clarisse and Bill?" he asks. Bill has come into the salon behind Clarisse. He touches her lightly on the shoulder and without looking at each other, they go in different directions.

"Yes," I say. "It seems odd that she's his daughter. There isn't a smidgeon of him in her."

"Exactly," Dick says.

"Is she adopted?" I ask. That thought had occurred to me before, but it seemed irrelevant.

"As a matter of fact she is adopted," Dick says. "But Bill Barnum isn't her father."

"He isn't?"

"No, he's her husband."

I swallow a couple of times trying to get my brain to work. "What do you mean?"

"I mean, he's her husband."

"But she's married to Meriodoc."

"What I mean is, he was her first husband. They divorced when she met Meriodoc who fell for her like a ton of bricks. She's so beautiful…" His voice gets small.

I wave my hand in front of his face.

"I'm finished with that, don't worry, Swanson. Anyway, Barnum had an opportunity to get Athena into France, but he couldn't get past Meriodoc who was insane on the subject of GMOs and anything that wasn't au terroir. Men get that way when they get older sometime. They want to make things right before they die."

"Okay, Dick." God, was Dick's heartbreak turning him into a philosopher?

"When Bill saw that Meriodoc was in love with Clarisse, he divorced her so she was free to marry him and use her influence to open the gates to Athena. She almost succeeded but Meriodoc wanted to be certain of her and he hired a private detective, a friend of mine in Paris, who found out that Clarisse was seeing Bill on the sly."

"Oh, dear. What about that résumé you gave me to read? Her life as a Hell's Angel meth queen. Where did you get that stuff from? It reads like a novel."

"She told me most of it, and most of it checks out, except the real daddy—or the adopted daddy—has been dead for more than ten years. That's when she left her home, such as it was, and became a waitress, then was abducted by the Angels. It's a tough story, even if the names have been changed."

I can see Clarisse in the salon, wearing a beautiful maroon velvet dress, smiling and talking to Guy who is bobbing his head all over the place like he's looking for something. Me, probably. She and Bill lock eyes once across the tables where people are waiting to be seated and I wonder how numb I had to be not to see their connection.

"You think Clarisse…?"

"Killed Meriodoc? Not unless she was stealing from him and he found out."

"Was she?"

"She wouldn't give me her financial disclosure papers for the divorce, so probably yes. Although she would have to be pretty stupid not to lie on those."

"What? What did you find out?" Dick asks me.

"Guy stole the divorce papers from me on the plane. I didn't forget them."

"How could someone steal from you when you were right there?"

"I was sleeping. With some help. Guy gave me a couple of sleeping pills." I felt like an idiot. Where was Euro woman? That was the fastest lifespan in the history of fantasy.

Dick sighs loudly.

"So what do you think?" I ask him.

"I think we shouldn't miss the fish course," he says. "Let's go into dinner and hope they serve a lot of wine. It's the only way to get people to reveal themselves."

Getting people to reveal themselves is a big Dick trick. I think he got it from his martial arts studies. His theory is that if you do nothing, eventually people will just confess. I have to admit, I've seen it happen more than once.

"Anyway," Dick says, "If we don't go in, whoever killed Meriodoc will think we found them out and perhaps do something desperate. Who knows what other mayhem they are capable of committing."

We are almost at the door when Dick offers me his arm and

says, "By the way, Swanson, the tuxedo is a very good look on you!"

Chapter 33

The Fish Was A Poem

Guy breaks away from Clarisse when he sees me enter the salon.

"You ran away from me! Where have you been?"

He touches my elbow, but I recoil.

"What's the matter?" he asks. "Aren't you the same person I just shared the best afternoon of my life with?"

The tables in the salon are full and I'm wondering are we going to eat dinner standing up when Clarisse opens the doors to an adjoining room and beckons to those of us standing to go in. After we have, she closes the doors to the salon. It's a smaller room but still grand and the dining table is set gorgeously. One end of the room is rounded like an alcove. The walls are slightly rounded and the dining table is round. There's a stairway in the wall that I assume leads down to the kitchen. Clarisse looks for Dick to pull out her chair and when he doesn't she seats herself, arching an eyebrow at him. I can't believe the enormity of her lie, telling people that Bill Barnum is her father. I think of Tulane's sideways reference to Barnum in the kitchen and wonder how much she knows but isn't telling.

Little cards tell us where to sit like we're at a wedding. Dick and Sébastien sit on either side of Clarisse. Sylvie and I are seated either side of Bill. Between Dick and me, is Guy. He takes his seat petulantly and I am glad there are all these people around because I know he wants to interrogate me.

"You look trés chic," Sylvie tells me. "You did it?" she asks Guy.

Guy looks at her glumly.

"Yes, he did it," I say. I want to smile at Guy, I really do, but I can't trust my feelings for him and I don't trust anybody at the table except Dick, who is talking to Clarisse in a matter-of-fact manner which obviously surprises her because she is used to slavish adulation from him. She touches his hand and whispers something in his ear, trying to make him smile. Good luck with that.

"He does that with all his girlfriends, makes them over," Sylvie says and even though I am leery of Guy I feel a sharp prick of jealousy. "He restyles them, he can't help it. It must make you feel as if you're not good enough." She smiles a spiteful smile at me.

"Shut up, Sylvie," Guy says. To me, "Is that why you're mad? You think I don't think you're good enough? What do I have to do to convince you?"

The butler places a small plate of poached salmon and caviar in front of each of us. I use my fork to change the position of the fish. Dick shoots me a look so I put the fork down. As soon as Clarisse picks up her fork the rest of us do.

Bill digs in and finishes the appetizer with a couple of bites. "Delicious, isn't it?" he asks me.

"Wonderful," I agree.

"Then why aren't you eating it?"

"I'm pacing myself. I'm assuming there's a lot more coming."

"You bet there is!" He leans back in his chair and rubs the western style shirt, complete with fringe that covers his belly. He waits for the sommelier to refill his wine glass and then he raises it in a toast. "We're all here for one reason, of course," he says. "And that's because Michel Meriodoc has passed."

"He was murdered," Dick reminds him.

"Yes, well, in the end it doesn't matter how, it only matters what, and the what is that the end has come for Michel Meriodoc." He pauses to see if Dick has a problem with that, and when he doesn't, Bill continues, "You all know that Michel and I agreed on a lot of things, mostly that Clarisse is the most wonderful girl in the world," he bows his head to Clarisse, "but we disagreed on one major thing and that was GMO food. Frankenfood, he called it. Now, I am a big admirer of Michel Meriodoc, but he was wrong about this. GMO food will make it possible to produce cheaper groceries for everyone in France and cheaper groceries mean no one will go hungry. I don't see any down side to that, do y'all?"

He makes a big arc with his glass around the table, challenging us to disagree with him. "Good. Well, the good news is that Sébastien has agreed to take on his father's mantel until the French Farmer's Association can meet to elect a new president probably by Christmas. He'll be the interim president as it were, and I intend to take advantage of the courage of this interim president to announce that Athena Food Corporation will begin to export GMO seed to France immediately."

"You can't be serious?" Sylvie says. "Is he serious?" she asks Sébastien. "Doesn't he know?"

"We've had a discussion, that's all," Sébastien says.

"This is absurd!" Sylvie says. "It's outrageous! We're developing it now."

"I'll say it's outrageous," Guy says. "You can't possibly hope to get away with this. You just told a whole plaza full of demonstrators that they should burn the seeds on the docks. I told everyone on my blog, which is the whole of France by the way, that you are against Athena GMO seeds. How are you going to explain this to them?"

"I told them I was against the importation of GMO seeds." Sébastien drinks his glass of wine in one gulp and snaps his fingers to have his glass refilled. "I have nothing against French GMO seeds."

Bill Barnum sits down, his face dark, and signals the sommelier to refill his glass. "I thought we were going to work together on this."

"I'm saying that I've already developed a GMO wheat seed that is native to France. We don't need to work with Athena. I don't need you. Barnum. Why should I let you come in and take my profits away from me?"

"I thought we had a deal? You can't back out of a deal."

"I've changed my mind, Barnum. I am the interim head of the French Farmers' Association and will be the elected head you can be sure, and I say that we only want French GMO seeds, not American modified organisms. The terroir movement is very big and growing and if the French found out that an American was involved they would boycott me. And as I am the only one who has developed a French wheat GMO, I will have a corner on the market. So, explain to me why I need you?"

"You Frenchies are always lecturing about morals. You can't go back on our deal. That's immoral."

Guy laughs. "You, Bill Barnum, are talking about morals? What about all the money that your daughter stole from Meriodoc?"

"What are you talking about, mister?"

"She skimmed all the cash she could out of this place and hid it in offshore accounts."

"How dare you insult me!" Clarisse says.

"Every time Meriodoc made a speech for 20,000 Euros he deposited the check in their joint account. Everytime Meriodoc endorsed a yogurt he deposited the check in their joint account. All the opportunities Meriodoc got because of the publicity I gave him, you stole the money, Clarisse. I didn't do what I did for your dead husband to make you rich. How dare you insult me!"

"I never did that!" Clarisse says. "I wouldn't even know how."

"But you did," Guy says. "This place is broke. In fact, it's up to its 15th century neck in debt."

"How can that be? I was counting on the money father made to pay off the loans I took out to finance my research. I owe so much money. Is this true, Clarisse?" Sébastien asks.

"Of course it's not true. How could I possibly do that?" She looks at Dick. "You saw my financials. I'm practically broke. I wasn't even going to ask Michel for a divorce settlement after I found out he got Tulane pregnant and I'm entitled to a lot. I have my reputation. You saw those statements, Dick. Tell them."

"You didn't give them to me," Dick says.

"Well, then you!" She stands up and points at me. "That's right. I gave them to you. I remember now. In your pathetic little office in Brookline."

"Hey!" I say. "It's not that little."

"Well, you took them," she says.

"Yes, I took them, but..." I am reluctant to accuse Guy. Even if he stole them from me, I can't point a finger at him in front of all these people.

Guy stands up. "I stole them from Swan," he says. "I admit it wasn't the right thing to do, but I wanted to know what had happened to all of Meriodoc's money. I am an heir too, as well as my sister, and I have a right to know."

"So," Clarisse says, "If you saw those papers, like you say you did, you saw that I am as poor as a church mouse. Zero assets. Zero cash. It's right there in black and white."

"True if I didn't look any further, but I did and what I saw are financial transactions in your name for close to 20 million Euros. That's what I saw." He rattles off the names of some banks in Belize and the Cayman Islands. "Any of those names sound familiar?"

"I never wrote those transactions down..." She puts her hand to her mouth and looks at Bill Barnum who looks like he is going to kill her. "I mean..."

"You didn't have to. Do you really think in the age of the hacker that anything is private? You might as well have been doing your banking in the middle of the Champs-Elysées. In less than an hour, I had everything. Unless," Guy looks sweetly at Clarisse, "perhaps I missed one?"

Bill Barnum throws his wine glass against the wall, startling us out of our torpor. He stands up and his chair falls backward. He looks so damned tall. "I'm going to kill you, you little twit," he says.

Guy gets out of his chair.

And runs.

Chapter 34

An Amazing Night

We all jump up just as the butler and two maids enter from the stairwell with steaming serving dishes. Bill is running after Guy who has sped through the double doors onto the terrace and vaults over the wall down onto the path that leads to the maze.

Clarisse is right behind them, screaming, "Bill, Bill, for God's sake, don't kill him Bill! Wait up, Bill!"

Sébastien runs out the door while he's throwing off his tux jacket, screaming, "I'm going to kill you, Clarisse! You two-bit American hustler."

I start after them too, although when you think about it they've revealed themselves, and only after one or two bottles of wine, and I'm not sure what my role in all this is now. Sylvie and Dick are the only ones who haven't joined the chase. I stop by Dick's chair. He smiles at me, scoops a sliver of poached salmon into his mouth, drains his wine glass and pushes his chair back. "That was easier than I thought it would be," he says then he trots out onto the terrace, vaults to the ground and starts after Sébastien. I watch him from the terrace wall. He bends forward and pumps his arms like a track star, something he probably was that he hasn't bothered to tell me about.

Sylvie strolls out onto the terrace and stands next to me observing. She hands me a Gauloise she's lit, shouts "Don't kill her before I get there, Sébastien! I want to kill her!" and bounds down the terrace steps in her skin tight dress.

Tulane comes out on the terrace with Chocolat and Piaf

144

leading the way and the three of them take the steps two at a time.

I feel like my heart is going to explode I am so happy that Guy confessed to stealing the file, that his motive was only wanting to know how much money he was going to lose or win back. I take off my pumps and run down the steps after them, yelling, "Run faster, Guy, run faster." I feel something nipping at my feet. "Devil Dog!" I cry. "Where did you come from? Come on! Let's go help Guy. We're coming, Guy!" and it's like I am flying through the garden as Devil Dog and I follow the moonlit figures down to the maze.

When a giant shadow crosses over us.

I stop and look up.

Hannibal!

"Jeezums," I say. "Not now."

Hannibal circles over us twice and Devil Dog starts to growl. Hannibal lets out a scream of recognition then glides away over the maze. Apparently tonight he has juicier pickings in mind.

Just ahead of us Sylvie tosses aside her shoes and disappears into the maze. Devil Dog and I stop at the trellised entrance and look at each other.

"You in?" I ask him.

He runs in and I follow.

Left right right, left right right. The sky is as perfectly blue black as it was last night, the moon is full, and the hedgerows and path through them are bathed in a frosty light. I feel like I'm running through a wedding cake. "Guy!" I yell. "Where are you Guy?"

"Yes, Guy, where are you?" Bill Barnum shouts from somewhere that sounds nearby but in a labyrinth a few feet away can be like a mile. "You little French twit, I'm going to crack open your pathetic French skull."

Devil Dog is barking as he runs. He seems to know where he's going and, since I don't, I follow him, barely keeping up. He comes to a dead end hedge wall but instead of coming back from it to find another way around he scrunches his body down and squirms under it. He paws at his side of the hedge and barks for me to follow. "Not even on a diet," I say, "Thanks a lot, boy." I hear him run off. Well, that's that, I think deflated, and start walking back in the direction we just came from and almost trip on him as he bursts through a break in the hedge wall and barks for me to follow. Which I do. We're in a section of the maze where the zigs and the zags are spaced further apart than at the beginning. I hear shouting and I turn left to see Dick and Sébastien. Dick has Sébastien's arms pinned behind him. "It won't do you any good to kill her. You'll only get yourself in worse trouble than you're probably in already."

"What are you saying?" Sébastien says.

"I'm not saying anything. I'm just telling you to cool down. I'm not going to let you go till you do."

Devil Dog has already disappeared through another opening. I run to catch up to him but he's stopped barking so I slow down and walk along a straight stretch of path, running my left hand along the hedges to make myself feel less disoriented. I hear voices ahead of me. I can tell they're whispering but the night air is so still and clear it's like an echo chamber and I can understand every word they're saying. It's Barnum and Clarisse.

"I told you to hide the money," Bill says.

"I did hide the money. What? Putting money in a Cayman island account isn't hiding it? What kind of a world are we living in?"

"It's these weird geeky kids. They're like aliens. They can find anything. I told you you were waiting too long to end it."

"I was waiting so it wouldn't look like I was in hurry. I thought I'd found the perfect cover."

The perfect cover! She meant Dick.

"What? Tulane being pregnant wasn't cover enough?"

"He only started the affair with her when he learned about us. You couldn't stay away. That's my fault?"

I hear Devil Dog barking for me and I turn to find him. "Wait for me, boy," I whisper.

"Who's there?" Bill yells. "Who's there?"

Devil Dog sits in the middle of the pathway I'm groping along, barks when he sees me, then runs out of sight. I hear barking besides his, follow the sound and come out in the fountain oasis I rested in last night. Tulane is sitting on my bench. Chocolat, Piaf, and Devil Dog are drinking from the fountain.

"Why did you come out here?" I ask.

"Why did you?"

"I'm trying to solve a murder."

"No you're not. You're trying to find Guy. You're in love with him even though he's a scoundrel."

"How do you know that I am?"

She laughs. "I told you that servants are the eyes and ears of a chateau. What I didn't see and hear myself, my staff did. I told Michel about Bill and Clarisse because I felt a sense of loyalty to him."

"You knew about that?"

"Of course!"

"And that's when your affair with him started?"

"Yes. Before that I don't think he even saw me. I mean me, not Tulane the housekeeper."

"It's that sexy French maid uniform."

"And then, suddenly, the uniform was off!" She pats her belly.

"*Bouf.* People like Clarisse get theirs in the end. She's already paid a high price for that stolen money just being with that oaf Bill Barnum."

I've been aware of Hannibal's gigantic shadow since we entered the maze. He's been circling silently. It's like he's looking for something.

"What are you going to do?" I ask Tulane. "If there isn't any money and no one wants to stay, the chateau will be sold. And the farm."

"I'll wait and see what happens. You never know. I don't worry about things I can't do anything about. Maybe this little person"—she pats her belly—"will have a say." Devil Dog has been running to the edge of the oasis and barking like he wants me to follow.

"I've got to find Guy," I say.

"Good luck," Tulane says. "He loves you, I think. He's visited here with other women, but you're different to him. I can see it."

Devil Dog barks for me to come and I follow. When this night ends Guy and I will pick up where we left off. I'm convinced that Bill Barnum killed Meriodoc. If he killed Meriodoc he was capable of killing Guy. I have to find him before Barnum does.

We go deeper and deeper into the maze and suddenly we come out into another open space, much bigger than the one where we left Tulane. This one has a wishing well in the middle surrounded by flowering bushes. Sylvie is on her knees digging with her bare hands in the bushes. Devil Dog runs up behind her and starts barking.

"Get lost, you mangy mutt!" she says and swipes at him. Devil Dog starts digging a few feet away from her.

"Goddamn gardeners," she says. "Turning over all the soil so I can't tell which side of the well I buried it in. She wipes her nose with the back of her hand, looks around and sees me.

"You!" she cries, getting to her feet. "Things were fine until you and that dick head friend of yours started mucking around in things that are none of your business."

"What do you care if you have nothing to hide? I would welcome the chance to be proven innocent."

"Nobody's innocent, you fool. Where do you Americans get such simplistic ideas? You think people get rich by hard work?"

She has a point. I've busted my ass for four years on the up-and-up and haven't much to show for it except shoes, a car and back rent.

"How come you hated your father-in-law so much? It wasn't like you and Sébastien were beggars."

"I hated his guts. He kept Sébastien chained down on that wretched farm collecting heirloom tomato seeds. He wanted the limelight to himself. When he found out Sébastien was developing authentic French GMO seeds and was going to market them as au terroir and that my brother was going to make him the new au terroir king on his blog, I thought he was going to have a heart attack. He threatened to give our farm to that trampy girl. Well, I wasn't going to let that happen."

She laughs like an insane person and pats Devil Dog who looks straight ahead with his tail at a ninety degree angle to the ground over the hole he has dug.

"What have you found, little hot dog?" she says. She reaches into his hole and picks up the rifle Devil Dog had dug up yesterday. "Goooood boy."

Devil Dog wags his tail like the sucker for European women he is. Sylvie opens the barrel and closes it with a snap.

Bill Barnum and Clarisse appear out of nowhere.

Sylvie raises the rifle sight to her left eye. "Not a step further," she says.

Bill laughs. "What are you going to do, Sylvie? Kill everyone who gets in your way like you killed Meriodoc? You're going to have to kill a lot of people because you've got the worst luck of anybody I've ever known."

"Shut up, Barnum. Your daughter stole my money and she's going to pay, one way or another."

"You think this is the way to get it?"

Sylvie lowers the rifle and extends her hand. "Okay, give it to me. All 20 million Euros."

"I don't know where that kook got that number," Clarisse says. "It's not even half that. Let's make a deal. We'll go fifty-fifty with you."

"That kook is my brother," Sylvie says, raising the rifle again.

"Well, I just can't hand you the money," Clarisse says. "I mean, I didn't hide it under a bed."

"What a pity." Sylvie cocks the trigger.

"Come on," Bill Barnum says. "We can settle this like friends. Sixty-forty. How's that sound?"

"You don't get it, do you," Sylvie says, pointing the gun at me. "Since this little busy-body and her friend arrived I don't have anything to lose."

"Hey, I have a job," I say, "I don't want any of your money."

Sylvie snorts. "Right. You'd be the first person on earth who didn't."

Hannibal has been circling overhead and it's like he finally sees what he's been looking for. The arc of his circles get tighter, his shadow bigger and darker.

"That damned crazy bird," Sylvie says. "I should just shoot it."

I remembered what Dick said when I arrived. If Hannibal could talk, he would tell us who the murderer was. He seems mighty interested in our little group.

Dick rushes into our circle pushing Sébastien. "Put that gun down, Sylvie. You look ridiculous," Dick says. "And take your husband home." He pushes Sébastien toward her.

"I'm not going back to that damned farm ever again," Sylvie says. "Why should you all get everything you want and I get nothing. I don't even get a husband who loves me. He worshipped his damned family name and cared more for a bunch of dirt than he ever cared for me. Isn't that right, Sébastien?"

"I'm not going to answer in front of all these people, Sylvie. You know I won't."

"See?" she asks us. "It's not a hard question to answer." She starts to cry and lowers the rifle a little. Bill Barnum rushes her and tries to wrest the gun away.

Just then Guy appears. "I've been following the sound of your voices. Finally, I've found you," he says. He sees me and runs to my side and hugs me.

"I am so sorry I didn't believe in you," I say. "I'm sorry I didn't read your blog. From now on…"

Guy puts his hand over my mouth to shut me up then takes it away and kisses me. I close my eyes for a second then open them to the sound of Hannibal screaming as he sinks his talons into Sylvie's neck. The gun goes off and the report echoes through the maze. Hannibal screams and flies off. Guy slips from my arms and falls to the ground.

Chapter 35

Is Greed A Crime Of Passion?

French detectives and agents from the French Interpol office were all over the chateau and they didn't know who to arrest first so they arrested everybody. Except Dick, of course—who performed secret international police handshakes with the French cops—who helped them round everybody up including Clarisse who pleaded with him to vouch for her, which he politely declined to do. That's the thing about Dick, about all policemen and detectives that I know, they may understand the complexities of the human heart and moral relativism, and even succumb to irrational emotions themselves, but at the end of the day, it's all about right and wrong. And what Clarisse did to Meriodoc—marry him to influence his decision about GMOs then filch all his money—isn't a moral gray area. It's pitch black.

Of course, you could argue that murder is the blackest of the black and I would agree. As Dick always says, that's one crime with no acceptable restitution. But they couldn't pin Meroidoc's murder on Clarisse. It was, as Hannibal eloquently pointed out, Sylvie.

Sylvie admitted to killing Meriodoc after an argument she and Sébastien and Meriodoc had in the garage after he threatened to sell the farm out from under them. There are rifles everywhere in a hunting chateau, as Theodore pointed out, including two against the wall in the berth where Meriodoc kept his Bentley. It seems understandable, if not inevitable, that someone reach for one when an argument becomes a Gordian knot. When the police were interrogating her, Sylvie kept yelling, "crime of passion," Dick said, but the French reserve that sobriquet for crimes about love.

Love. Let's not forget love.

No one will know who else Sylvie wanted to kill that night. Her husband, Sébastien, for not giving her the life she expected and worse, for slugging her when she pointed out his deficiencies to him? Clarisse for robbing her of her inheritance? Bill Barnum for attacking her in the maze? Me? For messing around and getting dangerously close to finding out the truth of her crime? They're all possible, of course, because who can figure the cracked logic of an insane person with grudges. But one thing is certain, she never meant to kill her beloved brother, Guy, who was the only person in the world who ever looked after her.

Dick told me that Guy knew Sylvie killed Meriodoc. She called him up after she did it and that's why he was on the plane with me. Not because Sébastien gave her another black eye, but because she didn't know what to do now that she had murdered her father-in-law. What if someone found out? Sébastien knew because he was there of course when it happened, and he was willing to give her up if the cops got too close to the truth. And she couldn't trust him not to give her up. It was likely him she was aiming at that night. We'll probably never know. And what does it matter? She killed Guy.

Guy. I am now fighting a feeling that I am jinxed in love. Worse, my lovers are jinxed. It would take a mighty powerful attraction to stick around after I tell any potential suitors that my last two boyfriends died in my arms because I was mucking around a murder case.

Did I love Guy? I could have. I was starting to. He opened up a side of me that I hadn't known was there: the sophisticated international woman with a marvelous lifestyle, who I am keen to discover. Since Devil Dog and I are staying in Paris with my uncles until they open Le Haut Dog, I have lots of opportunity to explore that part of me.

In fact, a week after the "hunt" in the maze, Uncle Joe wakes me up with a steaming bowl of café au lait and a piece of bread slathered with Nutella.

He sets the breakfast tray on the bottom of the bed and says, "It's here, Swanson."

"So I see," I say, "Bonjour!"

"No, not breakfast...."

Uncle Stevie sticks his head in my room. "Get out of bed, sleepy head! We have to go down to the docks. The diner's here!"

Chapter 36

Sometimes A Haut Dog Is Just A Hot Dog

Between solving the murder, getting to know the French countryside and my time with Guy, I haven't done a lot of sight-seeing in Paris. So I was thrilled that we were finally going to see the Seine at least. The diner was shipped from Boston in a container ship to Le Havre, loaded on a barge there to the port of Bonneuil-sur-Marne and reloaded there on a barge that is coming direct to the Port de la Bourdonnais which is right at the foot of the Eiffel Tower.

"See this is why the French are cool," Uncle Joe says. "They've got all these agencies to cooperate and devise a waterway system of transport to realize a 37% reduction of CO_2 emissions every year. We could never do that in Boston! We'd get tangled up in our own jock straps."

Another reason to hate France: they manage to do the right thing.

"I'm never going to really see Paris!" I complain from the back seat of Uncle Stevie's Citroën. I'm sure that once this diner unloads my uncles will be chained here.

"You'll have plenty of time for that. We need someone to help us get this restaurant up and moving," Uncle Stevie says.

"You don't expect me…"

"Why not you?"

"I'm a divorce lawyer."

"Yeah?" Uncle Joe looks at me the rear-view mirror. "How's

that working out?"

I slump down in my seat.

"Look, I think the barge is coming in now." He points through the windshield where a giant barge is coming into view.

We hastily and illegally park the car and run to the dock. It's an early autumn morning in Paris, France, and I am by the Eiffel Tower with the two people who are dearest to me in the world and my dog, who is barking with excitement, the same kind of excitement I'm feeling. My world is getting bigger. There's lots to bark at! To notice! And experience.

"I just hope you guys don't turn all Frenchy on me," I say.

"How could that ever happen?" Uncle Joe asks. "You travel and pick up the things you like about a place, and incorporate them into your life, but your core self? You always bring that with you."

"Maybe."

Uncle Joe and Uncle Stevie put their arms around my shoulders and as we squint into the rising sun, I can almost see the world as they see it and I am happy for them.

"We have Guy to thank for this," Uncle Stevie says.

"May his soul rest in peace," Uncle Joe says.

The barge pulls into the port and big trucks, which have been idling a couple of blocks away, drive down to the edge of the dock for the containers to be unloaded onto them. A flatbed truck is already parked there, probably for the diner.

There are three rows of containers and at the back of the barge is something gigantic covered with huge tarps which are secured to the barge with manila rope. It must be the diner underneath all that.

"That's it!" Uncle Joe yells, running towards it pointing.

A man on the barge sees Joe running towards the barge and pointing at the tarps. The man smiles and unties one of the ropes and then another till part of the building underneath is exposed. But it's not the silver railway-looking car I was expecting. It's a ratty looking structure covered in pink stucco, like a party boat you would see floating down the Ganges River.

"Hey," I say to Uncle Stevie, "That looks like..."

"The Southie Dunkin Donuts? Yeah, it is! Didn't Guy tell you? He got it for us immediately."

"But that's not a diner!"

"Underneath all that pink frosting, actually it is. You were too little to remember it before the Saads bought it and fixed it up for the franchise. It was an Irish luncheonette. The Barry family owned it. Didn't I ever tell you about Calsey Barry? She was the prettiest girl in Southie. Everyone was in love with her."

"Even you?"

"Especially me," he laughs.

A real American story. From Reuthenian men in love with Irish lassies to a Syrian family whose daughters were intent on going to college. I think of Max Oppenheimer and his wife and their bagel shop in Brookline. Jews who came from Germany and who are ready to move again if the future looked more promising somewhere else. My uncles moving to France. Maybe it isn't an exclusively American story all this moving in and out of places. It's a global story. And it's a good thing. The more you get to know people the more you like them. Look, I'm even getting fond of the French and I never in a million years thought that would happen. Maybe it took falling in love with a French man. I remember then I promised to send Max a postcard. "So this restaurant of yours..."

"Le Haut Dog."

"Yeah, Le Haut Dog, is going to be an authentic American experience. Au terroir as they say."

We walk down to the dock where Uncle Joe is already directing the men in the flatbed how to position their truck so the reach stacker can land the building on it in one try.

"I guess I don't have to go back to Boston immediately," I say.

"Atta girl," he says.

"I could do some consulting for you. What's authentic Boston, you know? What isn't. You know, define our lifestyle," I start to say, but stop myself and turn away so he doesn't see me cry. I snurf and turn back to him, and hand him a package that Tulane gave me "for luck" she said. It's a ceramic owl from Meriodoc's collection of owl statues which she showed me the day before I left. She wants my uncles to put it in their new restaurant. In fact, the owl that was on the passenger's seat of his car when he was murdered was one he had just bought at the flea market in Clignancourt earlier in the day. As Tulane said, just one fact doesn't tell you the whole story. "Just put it on the counter or something," I tell him, pushing the package in his hand and walking away.

"Hey, where ya going?" Uncle Joe asks.

When I told Max Oppenheimer I was going to France, he said, "Who wouldn't love France?" He was talking about love and at the time I wasn't listening, because I thought that part of my life was over. Wait till he finds out what happened to me.

"I have to buy a postcard," I say.

ABOUT THE AUTHOR

Bathsheba Monk is the creator of the Swanson Herbinko Mystery series. Read more about her on her website: www.bathshebamonk.com